SHOWDOWN AT WIDOW CREEK

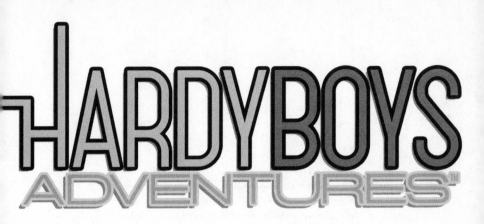

#11 *SHOWDOWN AT WIDOW CREEK*

FRANKLIN W. DIXON

ALADDIN   New York London Toronto Sydney New Delhi

ALADDIN

An imprint of Simon & Schuster Children's Publishing Division
1230 Avenue of the Americas, New York, NY 10020
This Aladdin hardcover edition February 2016
Text copyright © 2016 by Simon & Schuster, Inc.
Jacket illustration copyright © 2016 by Kevin Keele
Also available in an Aladdin paperback edition.
All rights reserved, including the right of reproduction in whole or in part in any form.
ALADDIN is a trademark of Simon & Schuster, Inc.,
and related logo is a registered trademark of Simon & Schuster, Inc.
THE HARDY BOYS MYSTERY STORIES, HARDY BOYS ADVENTURES,
and related logo are trademarks of Simon & Schuster, Inc.
For information about special discounts for bulk purchases, please contact
Simon & Schuster Special Sales at 1-866-506-1949 or business@simonandschuster.com.
The Simon & Schuster Speakers Bureau can bring authors to your live event.
For more information or to book an event contact the Simon & Schuster Speakers Bureau
at 1-866-248-3049 or visit our website at www.simonspeakers.com.
Jacket designed by Karin Paprocki
Interior designed by Mike Rosamilia
The text of this book was set in Adobe Caslon Pro.
Manufactured in the United States of America 0116 FFG
2 4 6 8 10 9 7 5 3 1
Library of Congress Control Number 2015943809
ISBN 978-1-4814-3878-0 (hc)
ISBN 978-1-4814-3877-3 (pbk)
ISBN 978-1-4814-3879-7 (eBook)

CONTENTS

THE HOLDUP

1

FRANK

TWO MASKED BANDITS DREW THEIR pistols as they closed in on a stagecoach. The lead desperado steadied himself in the saddle as he took careful aim at his target. The second did the same. Their pistols roared in unison as their horses galloped through white clouds of gun smoke.

"Heeyah!" shouted the driver. The portly man shook the reins, urging his four horses to run faster. He chanced a glance over his shoulder at the approaching outlaws. The driver turned back and shook the reins harder.

The man sitting next to the driver spun in his seat and aimed a shotgun at the villains. The gun roared, and flames erupted from both barrels. One of the gunmen flew from his saddle; the masked man tumbled to the ground.

"And that's why they call it 'riding shotgun,'" my brother, Joe, announced.

I rolled my eyes. "I know."

The other outlaw aimed his six-shooter and fired. The man riding shotgun dropped his weapon and fell from the top of the stage. He rolled to a stop in the soft dirt as the chase passed him by.

When the bandit fired again, the driver went down. The man slumped forward, dropping his reins. Now the stagecoach was running wild with no one to steer or stop it.

Suddenly one of the coach doors flew open. A cowboy wearing a white hat leaned out and blasted a six-shooter of his own. The remaining outlaw tumbled off the back of his horse.

"Ah! That's the good guy," said Joe. "You can tell because he's wearing a white hat."

I shushed him. "Do you mind?"

The cowboy holstered his pistol and climbed out of the cab. He scrambled up to the stagecoach's roof and made his way to the front. Without hesitation, the cowboy leaped onto the back of one of the coach's horses, then carefully stepped onto the rigging between the galloping steeds. Crouching low, he worked his way forward and grabbed the reins. He leaned back and pulled hard on the leather straps. Soon the runaway coach pulled to a complete stop.

The audience erupted in applause. Joe and I joined in

as the cowboy hopped to the ground and gave a long bow.

"I knew he'd stop the runaway coach," said Joe. "The good guy always wins."

Joe and I weren't sitting in a movie theater watching a western, though it felt like we were. (My brother likes to make comments throughout movies too, which drives me nuts.) No—Joe, Mom, Dad, Aunt Trudy, and I were sitting with most of Bayport in the bleachers of the high school stadium. We had the rare treat of watching Wally Welch's Rodeo and Wild West Show.

"Let's have another big round of applause for our players," boomed the announcer's voice. "And if you want to throw in a couple of *yee-haw*s, we won't hold it against ya!"

Several members of the audience were happy to oblige, including my brother.

The two outlaws, already back on their horses, waved to the cheering spectators. The man riding shotgun had climbed back onto the coach and waved as well. The hero cowboy sat on the back of one of the horses and tipped his white hat to the crowd.

"And don't worry, folks, our driver is just fine," the announcer continued. "In fact, that's none other than our head honcho himself, Mr. Wally Welch!"

The driver came out of his slump, reins in hand. "Yee-haw!" he shouted as he slapped the reins onto the horses' backs. The animals bolted forward into a gallop, pulling the stagecoach around the stadium in a victory lap. As it passed the bleachers, Wally Welch waved to the crowd, a wide grin spread across his gray-bearded face.

The stagecoach had never been in danger of running wild. During the entire chase, it had made the same wide circle around the dirt-covered center of the stadium. The entire field had been modified for the event. Truckloads of dirt had been carted in, and temporary metal fence panels surrounded the area. A couple of cowboys swung open two of those panels, allowing the stagecoach and riders to exit the field.

"Pretty cool, huh?" asked Joe. "Aren't you glad I talked you into coming?"

"Yeah," I replied. "You have me there."

This wasn't our usual Friday night out. If one of us didn't have a date, you could usually find my brother and me hanging out with our friends at the Chomp and Chew— the diner with the best hamburgers in Bayport. Of course tonight most of our friends were at the show (a point Joe had made to get me here).

Plus, how often does Bayport get to see an honest-to-goodness rodeo? Joe had always been more of a westerns fan than me, but I had to admit that I was enjoying the show. We had seen trick roping, bronc busting (cowboys trying to stay atop a bucking horse), and a few other historical reenactments like the stagecoach robbery.

"Next up, folks," boomed the announcer's voice, "our top ranch hand and Wally Welch's daughter herself. Let's hear a big welcome for Sarah Welch and Hondo!"

The audience applauded as a young girl rode into the stadium. She looked to be about seventeen and rode a large brown-and-white horse. Her auburn hair was pulled back into a long braid. She kicked her horse into a gallop and began a loop around the field.

"Hondo's a pinto," said Joe. "Or what they call a paint— the same kind of horse Tonto rode in *The Lone Ranger*."

"Uh-huh," was all I could reply. I have to admit, I was instantly enamored with Sarah Welch. Even from several yards away I could tell she was pretty cute.

And, as it turned out, she was quite talented, too.

Once Hondo had reached a steady pace, Sarah kicked her boots out of the stirrups and hopped onto the seat of the saddle. She slowly stood straight as the horse continued to gallop. The audience cheered at the sight. Sarah then dropped to a seated position with both legs draped over one side of the saddle. For a few gallops, she rode sidesaddle, the way ladies wearing long skirts used to ride.

Sarah had a unique saddle. Instead of the usual short saddle horn protruding from the top, hers seemed to be about a foot long. It was thin and wrapped with tape.

She didn't ride sidesaddle for long. She grabbed the saddle horn with both hands and slid off the horse. Both feet hit the ground and her legs shot up and back. Still holding the horn, she swung her body over the back of the horse until her boots hit the ground on the other side of the horse. Once again, she used the ground to propel herself up. Her legs scissored wide as they flew across the horse.

The audience cheered even more.

"Just like a pommel horse," said Joe.

He was right. Sarah moved her body around Hondo similar to the way a gymnast would train on a pommel horse, only Sarah's moves were more impressive because a pommel doesn't gallop around a stadium.

Sarah continued to perform breathtaking moves atop the loping horse. With her back pressed against the animal's side, she raised both legs straight out. Then, back on the saddle, she stood on one leg with her other leg pulled up behind her. After each elegant maneuver, she would easily drop back into the saddle as if it were nothing.

As her performance ended, Sarah put a foot in a stirrup and hooked the other behind the tall saddle horn. She extended her body so that it was perpendicular to the horse. She spread her arms as they moved around the field one last time and waved to the audience.

"How about another hand for Sarah Welch," urged the announcer. The audience didn't have to be asked twice. They cheered wildly as Sarah galloped off the field.

"I'm going to hit the concession stand," I said, standing up. "Does anyone want anything?"

"No, thank you," said my dad. The rest of my family shook their heads. Everyone but Joe, who also rose to his feet.

"I'll join you," he said with a grin.

I sighed. There was no fooling him.

Once we were out of earshot of the family, he leaned in. "So, how are you going to do it?"

"Do what?" I asked, stepping down the bleachers toward the walkway.

"Meet Sarah," he replied.

"I just want to congratulate her," I said.

"Sure." My brother rolled his eyes. "Welcome her to Bayport. See how long she'll be in town. Maybe take her out for coffee."

I shrugged. "Maybe something like that."

"Don't worry about me," Joe assured. "I'll just blend into the background. And hey, maybe I can meet one of those stagecoach guys, learn how they did those tricks."

We walked past the concession stand toward the back of the stadium. On the way we passed several livestock trailers, a covered wagon, and the stagecoach we saw earlier.

"She must be close." Joe pointed. "There's her horse."

Two cowboys led the brown-and-white horse past us. I figured they were performers since they had bandannas covering their faces. However, for such a well-trained horse, Hondo seemed to resist being led.

After a few more steps, I stopped. Something wasn't right. The masked men weren't the same ones we'd seen in the show. These cowboys weren't dressed in flashy shirts and vests like the ones in the rodeo. And why would the performers still be wearing bandannas over their faces—especially in the midday heat?

"What's up, bro?" asked Joe.

Before I could reply, I heard a horse neigh behind us. Joe and I turned to see the men trying to lead Hondo into a trailer. The horse reared back and shook his head. One masked man held fast to the lead rope, while the other smacked the horse's rump with his hat.

"Something seem strange to you?" I asked.

Joe chuckled. "What? You think those are *real* bandits just because their faces are covered?"

The horse neighed once more before finally entering the trailer. The men shut the door behind the reluctant horse.

"Wait," said Joe. "Those aren't the same guys from the show."

Finally my brother had reached the same conclusion as I had.

"I bet those are *real* horse thieves."

OUTLAWS 2

JOE

H EY!" FRANK SHOUTED AS HE JOGGED toward the men and the trailer.

I kept pace with my brother. "Can we talk to you for a second?"

I couldn't make out anything about the men's faces but their eyes. And those eyes widened as we moved toward them. They left the back of the trailer and ran ahead to the old pickup truck the trailer was hitched to, quickly jumping inside.

"Those are definitely horse thieves," I said as we broke into a run after them.

The truck tried to start as Frank ran to the driver's door. "What are you doing?" he asked, beating on the side of the truck. The engine whirred again but didn't catch.

Instead of moving to the passenger door, I made a beeline for the front of the trailer. Luckily, I knew my way around trailer hitches. I unhooked the safety chain and popped the clasp locking the trailer's cup over the ball hitch on the back of the truck.

The truck tried to start again, but the engine still didn't turn over. That was good for me. The last place I needed to be was in front of that trailer when it began moving. And that's where I was. I was busy cracking away, lowering the stand so the trailer's tongue would be raised above the ball hitch. It's a painfully slow process—and by painfully, I mean that the muscles in my shoulder were burning as I spun the crank.

Frank beat on the side of the truck again. "Come out for a second. We just want to talk to you."

The truck starter whirred a final time before catching and roaring to life. I leaped to the side as the tires spun out and the truck pulled away, covering me with dirt. Luckily, I had raised the trailer's tongue just enough so that the trailer stayed put. The horse whinnied and stomped around inside.

"If that was a thank-you, then you're welcome," I told the horse.

"What's going on here?" asked a man running toward us. I recognized him from the show as Wally Welch.

"I think someone was trying to steal your horse," replied Frank. "Or your daughter's horse."

We explained what had happened to Mr. Welch and a few of his ranch hands who had gathered nearby. Two of the men led the horse out of its trailer, while another went for the police. Luckily, since most of Bayport was at the show that night, the cops had excellent response time. Little did I know that one of those cops was someone we could've done without seeing. It was the chief of police himself, Chief Olaf.

"Well, look who it is," said the chief as he strolled up to the scene. "The brothers Hardy. Somehow always at the scene of the crime."

My older brother and I didn't have the best relationship with Chief Olaf. Actually, we didn't have the best relationship with *Officer* Olaf, way before he became chief of police. See, we've been solving mysteries of one kind or another since we were eight and nine years old. Our father used to be a detective, so I guess it's in our blood. Unfortunately, it didn't look good for the Bayport Police—or its chief—when their cases were solved by a couple of kids. Frank and I had always had an understanding with the former chief of police. But now that Olaf was in charge, we had to keep our sleuthing way, *way* under the radar.

Mr. Welch clapped a hand on each of our shoulders. "These two thwarted the plans of a couple of no-good horse thieves."

Olaf eyed us suspiciously. "Is that right?"

I shrugged. "No big deal. Just happened to be in the right place at the right time."

The chief stared at Frank. "And just what were you two doing back here, at the right time?"

I caught my brother's eye. *Dude, don't say we were on our way to the concession stand.* That excuse hadn't worked on me, and it sure wouldn't work on Olaf, especially since the concession stand was on the other side of the stadium.

"I, uh . . . wanted to meet Sarah Welch," Frank admitted.

I was surprised that he went with the truth.

"Who wanted to meet me?" asked a girl's voice. We turned and saw Sarah Welch walk up with a couple of ranch hands. "And what's this about someone trying to steal Hondo?"

Frank raised a hand. "I—uh—we were back here when we saw two guys trying to take him in that trailer."

"And these boys stopped them," Mr. Welch said proudly.

Sarah took Hondo's halter and scratched the top of his head. She turned back to us. "If that's true, then thank you very much."

"You're welcome." Frank held out a hand. "I'm Frank Hardy, by the way."

I waved. "And I'm his brother, Joe."

Olaf sighed. "All right, boys. Tell us what happened." A uniformed police officer joined the chief. The woman pulled out a pen and small tablet to take notes as Frank and I retold the story.

"Descriptions?" asked the woman.

"They both wore bandannas over their faces," Frank explained. "But the driver wore an orange plaid shirt and had blond hair. He had on a black bandanna."

Mr. Welch screwed up his face. "You think it could be Mike Sullivan, Lucky?"

A tall, thin cowboy with a handlebar mustache nodded. I recognized him as the hero from the stagecoach robbery. "That might be him. You could spot that shirt clear across the ranch."

"The other guy had dark hair," I added. "And he wore a brown shirt and a red bandanna."

Lucky sighed and shook his head. "If one's Mike, then the other would be his brother, Tim."

"You know them?" asked Olaf.

Mr. Welch nodded. "Two of my latest hires."

"What about the vehicle?" asked the officer.

Frank described the old green-and-white truck.

"That's one of mine," said Mr. Welch. "Not only are they horse thieves, but they're truck thieves too."

"That makes us shorthanded for the cattle drive back to the ranch," Lucky said. "We might have to cancel this one."

"Cattle drive?" Frank asked. "Really?"

"Oh, yeah," said Sarah. "We drive a small herd all the way back to the Double W after every show. It's about twenty-five miles from Bayport, so this one will be a short, two-day drive."

"Cool," I said. That actually sounded like a lot of fun.

"Well." Chief Olaf peered at us. "Have you boys ridden horses before?"

"Sure," replied Frank. "A few times back in summer camp."

The chief grinned. "Well, Mr. Welch, I think I found a couple of replacements for you."

Frank's eyes widened. "What?"

"Sweet!" I said.

"Great idea," Sarah said, turning to me. "People pay us to ride in a real cattle drive. Not only would you be helping us out, but it would be a way to thank you for rescuing Hondo."

"I—uh—" Frank stammered.

I couldn't believe what a great opportunity this was. As a huge fan of old western movies, I'd jump at the chance to play cowboy and pretend to drive a herd of cattle across the country. Heck, *I'd* pay for it. "We'd have to ask our parents," I said. "But count us in!"

Frank's brow furrowed. "Um . . ."

"Well, if it's all right with them, we can have you back in Bayport by Sunday afternoon," Welch said.

"You'll also be doing me a favor, Mr. Welch," Olaf explained. "A weekend without the Hardy boys will give me one less thing to worry about." He turned and walked toward the parking lot.

Sarah nudged Frank. "In trouble with the law, huh? You'll have to tell me about that during the trip." She smiled and led Hondo away.

While the crowd dispersed, I leaned close to my older brother. "Pretty cool, huh?"

Frank shook his head. "I feel like the cowboy who has been run out of town by the local sheriff."

MOVE 'EM OUT 3

FRANK

A LITTLE AFTER EIGHT THAT NIGHT, with a trunk full of camping gear and extra clothes, I pulled out of our driveway and drove back to the stadium. The plan was to camp there for the night before heading out first thing in the morning. Of course our parents gave us permission. Joe had promised (for both of us, I might add) that we'd double up on our chores the following weekend.

"This is going to be so cool, bro," Joe said from the passenger seat. "A real cattle drive."

I rolled my eyes. "Oh, yeah."

Okay, I had to admit that I was more excited than I was letting on. It wasn't every day that we got the opportunity to get a small taste of what it was like to live as a cowboy. I

15

could even see why some people paid for the opportunity. I guess it weirded me out that we had been bullied into it by the chief of police.

"Hey, you wanted to meet Sarah." Joe threw up his hands "And now you get to hang out with her for the entire weekend."

"True," I agreed. "As long as I don't fall off my horse in front of her." I glanced over at him. "Summer camp was a long time ago."

Joe waved me away. "It'll be just like riding a bike."

"Sure," I replied. "A bike with a mind of its own that can buck you off whenever it feels like it."

We pulled into the empty stadium parking lot and parked near an open meadow on the side. That seemed to be where we would camp for the night. A few campfires lit small groups of people sitting around them. Nearby was a covered wagon and a row of horses tied to a rope that ran between two stakes driven into the ground.

We got out of the car and I popped the trunk. While Joe and I pulled our packs out, two figures left one of the campfires and walked over to us.

"Glad you could make it," said Wally Welch.

Sarah smiled. "I wasn't sure if you would."

"We wouldn't miss this, Mr. Welch," said Joe.

"You're official ranch hands now," he replied. "Call me Wally like everyone else."

Sarah waved us over. "Come on. We'll show you where to stow your gear."

She and Wally led us to the covered wagon, and we heaved our packs over the side.

"Go ahead and stow your car keys, son," Wally suggested. "You don't want to lose them on the trail."

"Good idea." I zipped up my keys into one of my pack's side pockets.

"And your cell phones," added Sarah.

Joe's jaw dropped. "Really?"

Wally grinned. "We do our best to be as authentic as possible. We can't have the latest pop song ringtone stirring up the herd."

Sarah raised an eyebrow. "And no texting while cattle driving."

I couldn't help but smile as I pulled out my phone and powered it down. Joe did the same. I knew that my brother would feel naked without his phone. But hey, he wanted to see what life was like in the Old West.

I opened the top of my pack. "We brought sleeping bags," I said. "Where are we camping?"

"No need for those, Frank," Wally said. "We'll bring them along in case there's a cold snap, but if the weather's nice, we'll bunk down just like the cowboys did back in the day."

Now it was my turn to feel a bit uneasy. I didn't know what the sleeping arrangements would be, but I bet not as comfy as my down-filled sleeping bag.

After stowing our gear, Wally and Sarah led us to one of

the dwindling campfires. It looked as if everyone had just turned in for the night—the other two campfires had dark shapes lying next to them. As we approached the third fire, two figures stood and joined us in the firelight.

"This is Ned and Dusty," said Wally. "Boys, this is Frank and Joe Hardy. They're here to help us drive the cattle back to the ranch."

Ned was a short, stocky man with black hair and a dark, bushy beard. "Good to meet you," he said as he shook our hands.

Dusty must have gotten his name from his mop of dirty blond hair. He was a foot taller than Ned and wore denim overalls. A toothpick jutted from the corner of his mouth. "We got your bunks all laid out." He pointed to two blankets spread out beside the campfire.

The old, thin blankets looked as if they came from an army surplus store—Confederate Army, maybe. Instead of a pillow, each spread was topped with an old saddle.

I pointed to the blankets. "This is us?"

Wally slapped me on the back. "Get some shut-eye, boys. We pull out at first light."

"Good night," said Sarah. "And thanks again." She followed her father out of the firelight.

I don't know if Sarah was thanking us for saving her horse or for helping with the cattle drive. Either way, my mind was with my soft bed back at home.

Ned and Dusty stretched out on their nearby blankets.

"It may not seem like much now," said Ned. "But after a day on a cattle drive, this is going to seem like a five-star hotel."

"That's the truth," agreed Dusty.

Joe and I took our places next to the campfire. I propped myself up on one elbow and watched as Joe tried to get comfortable on the hard ground. "Still living the dream?" I asked.

Joe adjusted the saddle under his head. "What's not to like?"

I lay back on the saddle and shifted enough that I hoped I wouldn't wake with a stiff neck. I looked up at the sky. A few stars winked above. Wally was right. The weather was warm and breezy, and it was a perfect night to sleep under the stars. It wasn't the first time that my brother and I had been camping without a tent. However, when I finally drifted to sleep, I dreamed of my sleeping bag just a few feet away in the covered wagon.

"Rise and shine!" said a voice in my dream as a rude clanking noise sounded nearby.

My eyes popped open. Wally strolled through the camp, clanking a spoon against a blackened coffeepot.

"It's still dark," Joe said as he rubbed his eyes. "Didn't we just go to sleep?"

"Nope," replied Dusty as he tied his rolled blanket to the back of his saddle. "It just seems like it."

"I thought we were getting up at first light," I said.

"Wally said we're *heading out* at first light," said Ned. He jutted a thumb over his shoulder. "And first light is coming up fast."

As my eyes adjusted, I saw that it wasn't as dark as I had thought. The sky was indeed lighter in the east.

Ned and Dusty showed us how to roll up our blankets and attach them to the back of our saddles. After that, they introduced us to our companions for the weekend—our horses.

Ned pointed to a brown horse with patches of white on his feet. "Frank, this'll be your horse—and he's a good one. This is Harvey."

"Harvey?" asked Joe.

"That's right," replied Dusty. He removed his toothpick and pointed to the tan horse next to him. "This one's yours. Meet Norman."

"Norman?" Joe repeated. "I thought cowboy horses were supposed to have cool names like Trigger, Silver, or Blaze."

Dusty returned the toothpick to his mouth and pretended to cover Norman's ears. "Hush, now. You'll hurt his feelings."

Ned smiled. "Yeah, you run a ranch for so long, you kind of go through those kinds of names quick."

After Joe and I got a crash course in saddling our horses, we joined everyone at the chuck wagon for a quick breakfast.

"How'd you sleep?" asked Sarah. She handed us each a metal plate full of bacon and eggs.

I rubbed the back of my neck. "Just great."

Sarah smiled. "You'll get used to it."

During breakfast, we ran into the three people who'd paid to be a part of the cattle drive. There was Mr. and Mrs. Mueller, who had just moved to Bayport from New York. And then there was Tom Jackson, whom we already knew. He was the assistant manager at the H&T grocery store in town.

After breakfast we were issued genuine cowboy boots, hats, and a couple of bandannas.

I held up mine. "We're not going to rob a stagecoach on the way, are we?"

Wally laughed. "No, but it keeps the sun off your neck, the dust out of your nose, and the sweat off your brow. Think of it as the cowboy Swiss army knife."

"What about our six-shooters?" Joe asked. He mimed a quick draw.

Wally rolled his eyes. "Contrary to what Hollywood tells you, the average cowboy doesn't ride with a gun on cattle drives. Unless, of course, they are traveling through hostile territory, which, I assure you, we are not."

Once we were fully equipped, we got a quick riding lesson. There, we met the third ranch hand who would be accompanying us on the drive. It was Lucky, the man Joe and I had met the night before. He eyed his students from under a dusty black hat. The bright white hat from the night before must've been just for show.

"Now, don't be timid," he instructed. "These horses are all well trained. But if they think you're a pushover, they *will* take advantage of you." A smile spread under his handlebar mustache. "A little slow to get going here, stopping to graze there, and pretty soon, they'll want to ride you." Everyone laughed. "All right, let's do a few laps around camp."

It wasn't quite like riding a bike, but most of it did come back to me. The only thing I forgot was to stand up in the stirrups when the horse broke into a trot. This was to keep my seat from slapping against the saddle. But a little pain helped me remember right away.

Joe, on the other hand, was a natural. He wore a wide grin as Norman broke into a trot beneath him.

When we were almost finished, Sarah rode up on Hondo. "How does everyone feel?"

"Raring to go," Joe replied.

"Good," she said. "Because it's time to move 'em out."

Once everyone was in position, the ranch hands opened a large pen and the cattle filed out. There were about one hundred of them, and twenty riders total. The ten extra cowboys were there just to help us get out of Bayport. Later, they would ride back to the stadium, break down all the equipment, and head to the next town. Apparently the ten of us would be more than enough to drive the herd back to the ranch.

With a couple of police cars diverting traffic, we drove the cattle out of Bayport along less-used side streets. I'm sure we made for quite a sight. And Joe and I had front-row seats . . . or back-row seats. We brought up the rear with only the chuck wagon rolling behind us, driven by Wally and pulled by a pair of mules.

With the extra cowboys keeping the herd in the center of the streets, we slowly made our way through less and less populated areas. Soon we were traveling down a two-lane blacktop in a more rural area just outside of town.

As we traveled farther, Sarah and Hondo waited on the shoulder, then fell into step beside us.

"How do you like riding drag?" she asked.

"Excuse me?" I asked.

"Riding behind the herd," she explained. "All the green-horns start out riding drag."

Joe jutted a thumb to himself and then to me. "That's us. We're the greenhorns."

"Why do we—the greenhorns—start in the back?" I asked.

"Because you don't have to do much, to be honest," she said. "Just drive the stragglers forward. But on a real cattle drive, riding across the dry plains, the back is the dustiest place to be."

"Not to mention the land mines that the cows leave behind," Joe added.

Sarah laughed. "There is that, for sure. But don't worry. We're almost to the good part."

"Oh, yeah?" I asked.

"We're about to reach the first ranch," she explained. "From here on out, we cut through different ranches until we get to ours. That way we'll be off the streets so it'll feel more like a real cattle drive."

"Cool," said Joe.

True to her word, we rounded a bend and saw the cattle file through an open gate. The cows immediately spread out and began grazing on the lush grass.

Once we were all through, including the wagon, Dusty closed the gate and waved at the departing ranch hands, who turned and rode back toward town.

"Now, this is more like it," said Joe.

It was pretty cool. It wasn't quite the open plains, but the large pasture made it seem like we were in cattle country.

Joe nudged the sides of his horse. He held out his hat as his mount broke into a trot.

Then the horse began to buck. Joe dropped his hat and held on to the saddle horn with both hands. The horse bucked even more, and Joe flew off the horse!

HOLD YOUR HORSES

4

JOE

NE MOMENT I'M CLINT EASTWOOD, riding across the open prairie, and the next I'm Joe Hardy, flying off the back of my horse.

Okay, so it didn't happen as fast as that. I kicked Norman into a trot, and then a lope, when I felt a pop vibrate through the saddle. Norman must not have liked it, because he began to buck. *That's* when I experienced the whole flying-off-my-horse thing. Not so fun.

I hit the ground hard, landing on my hip. Even though the pain was agonizing, I was aware of my situation well enough to roll away from the jumping horse. Norman bucked his way into the grazing herd of cattle. His saddle slid to his side with only the chest straps and belly strap holding it in place. Those straps didn't hold for long, though. Norman moved around so much that the thin straps snapped and the horse trampled the saddle under his hooves. The saddle and blanket stayed on the ground while the horse bucked away. He kicked a few more times before coming to a stop.

As I lay on the ground moaning, I heard galloping hooves approach. Sarah and Frank rode up to where I'd fallen. They slid off their horses and bent over me.

"Joe, are you all right?" asked Frank.

"Hang on!" I ordered. "Don't touch me." I waited for the throbbing in my hip to subside.

Sarah walked over to my saddle, then examined it. "The cinch broke," she reported.

The cinch was the main strap keeping the saddle on the back of a horse. Only the worst thing to break.

"Hopefully that's all that's broken," I grunted. The throbbing eased a bit, and I reached toward my brother. "What are you doing?" I asked. "Don't just stand there; help me up."

Frank helped me to my feet. I rubbed my sore hip.

"Think you broke anything?" Frank asked.

I shook my head. "But there's going to be a whopper of a bruise."

"Wait a minute," said Sarah. She unbuckled the cinch and examined it more closely. "This didn't break on its own. Someone cut it."

"What?" I asked.

Sarah dropped the strap and raised her arms. "Everyone

stop where you are," she ordered. "Lucky! Check everyone's cinch straps."

"You got it," Lucky replied. He slid off his horse and began ducking under the other riders' horses.

Wally pulled the chuck wagon close. "Frank, get Joe to the back of the wagon," he said. "Then help Lucky check those straps, starting with yours."

"I can make it the rest of the way," I told my brother. "Go on and help."

He stared at me with worry in his eyes. "You sure?"

I smiled. "I'm fine, bro."

I limped to the back of the wagon, wincing in pain as I climbed in. It was a good thing Frank wasn't around to see that; I'd never get rid of him.

Wally climbed out of the driver's seat and joined me. "How do you feel, son? Think you broke anything?"

Why did everybody keep asking me that? Now I wasn't so sure.

"I don't think so," I said, twisting at the waist.

Wally chuckled. "Well, if you did, you wouldn't be able to do that without screaming like a bobcat. Though I'll wager you'll be stiff as blazes tomorrow."

Sarah, Frank, and the other ranch hands strode over to us. They each dropped a cinch strap into the back of the wagon.

"Every last one of them is cut," said Lucky. He picked up one of the straps and pointed. Each strap was made from several rows of small, soft rope. Lucky pointed out a thin cut crossing all the strands; each rope was almost sliced in half. "I'm surprised it took this long for one to go," he added.

"Every one is cut but mine and Lucky's," said Sarah. "We both have solid straps."

"There's a feed store about five miles from here," Lucky said. "I can ride over there and get us some more straps."

Wally tightened his lips and shook his head. "No, that'll put us too far behind schedule." He opened a nearby wooden crate and pulled out another cinch, looking it over before tossing it to my brother. "Frank, re-saddle your horse, then help Sarah and Lucky round up the cattle."

Frank glanced at Ned and Dusty. "Wouldn't someone with more experience be better for that?"

Wally smiled. "Fine. What's your experience repairing cinch straps?"

Frank shook his head. "None."

"That's what I thought," said Wally. "The boys will stay here and help with that while you get some on-the-job training rounding up strays. Less of a learning curve in that department."

"Yes, sir," said Frank. He followed Lucky and Sarah back to the horses.

Ned and Dusty grabbed a couple of straps each and strode over to Mr. Jackson and the Muellers. "Lots of things can happen on the trail, folks," Dusty announced. "Today's first lesson is a cowboy quick fix."

While the ranch hands took care of the paying guests, Wally dug a pocketknife out of his pocket and began to cut the cinches all the way through. "I'll show you how to tie these back together. There are a couple of knots that should hold enough for us to get back to the ranch."

Wally showed me how to tie the knots; I watched him carefully, trying to mimic the same technique. But all the while, the question on my mind was the one no one had asked. So finally, I asked it. "Who would cut all the straps?"

Wally stopped working. "I've been pondering the same question. I know Mike and Tim tried to steal Hondo, but why would they cut our cinches, too? It's not like we'd chase them on horseback."

"That's a good point," I said. I untied my clumsy knot and tried again. "The motive isn't clear."

"Motive?" Wally asked. "Like in a mystery?"

"Well, sure," I replied. "Every crime has a motive, such as money or revenge."

Wally grinned. "Sounds like you watch a lot of those true-crime shows."

"Not really," I replied. "Well, I do, but that's not why I know so much about mysteries. You see, my brother and I are kind of detectives." I went on to give him the brief history of all things Hardy—from our retired detective father to the real reason why Chief Olaf volunteered us for the cattle drive.

Wally Welch gave a hearty belly laugh, and the whole

wagon shook. "You two must have been a real bur under his saddle for him to hold a grudge that long."

"If that means what I think it means, sir, then yes," I said. "We're not on the best of terms with the chief."

"Well, you seem okay in my book," said Wally. "And if you boys can put your heads together and find out who's behind this mess, I'd be much obliged."

"I'll see what we can do," I said with a smile of my own.

Wait until I tell Frank, I thought. A cowboy vacation *and* a mystery!

5

ROUND 'EM UP

FRANK

I COULD FEEL IT IN THE AIR. NO, I COULD SMELL it. At the other end of the pasture, my brother was already trying to solve the mystery of the sabotaged cinch straps. We're not twins, and we don't have any kind of brotherly psychic link, but I could just tell.

It was a no-brainer, really. Someone had cut the straps, but no one had had time to question it because the drive had to go on. But if I knew Joe Hardy, even injured, he'd already begun asking questions and creating a suspect list. I hated to admit it, but I was thinking the same thing.

Of course, I would've been putting more thought into it if I wasn't galloping after a wayward calf. The brown-and-white animal bawled for his mother as he ran into a grove of trees.

"Wait here," said Lucky. "I'll go after him. And when he comes out, try to steer him toward the rest of the herd."

"You got it," I said. I rode my horse into a gap leading to another open field and brought him to a stop. Harvey pawed at the ground with one hoof, anxious to continue the chase. "Whoa, boy," I told him.

Lucky rode into the trees after the calf. I heard twigs snap and the sounds of hooves on dry leaves. Then, a few moments later, the little calf bolted out of the tree line and ran straight for me. If he got past me and into the open clearing behind me, we'd be chasing him all day.

I took off my hat and waved it over my head. "Hee-yah!" I shouted, trying to sound like the cowboys I'd seen in movies. The calf didn't seem to care; he just kept coming, veering off to one side to get around me.

I was about to kick Harvey into action. Oddly enough, I didn't have to. The horse turned on his own, blocking the calf's escape. This just caused the calf to slide to a stop and break around the other side. Harvey wasn't having it. The horse sidestepped and blocked his path there as well. Harvey moved so quickly that I had to grab the saddle horn to keep from falling off. After one more thwarted attempt, the calf finally turned and ran in the opposite direction—luckily, where the rest of the herd was grazing.

"Good job," said Lucky as he rode out of the tree line. He ducked under a branch as he moved closer.

"I wish I could take credit for it," I told him. I patted my horse on the shoulder. "But this one was all Harvey."

Lucky smiled. "I guess I should've warned you. Harvey was a cutting horse in his prime."

"A cutting horse?" I asked.

"That's a horse that's been trained to cut cows away from the rest of the herd," Lucky explained. "The good ones can turn on a dime, blocking a cow as it tries to get past. A good cutting horse can match a cow's movements, step for step."

I patted Harvey again. "So it came back to you just like riding a bike, huh, boy?"

Lucky kicked his horse. "Come on. Let's follow this one back to the herd and see if Sarah needs help."

We rode alongside each other while the calf walked ahead of us. Lucky explained more about cutting horses and mentioned that Harvey had won a few awards in his day.

"And all with a name like Harvey," I said.

Lucky laughed. "You said it."

While I still had Lucky alone, I thought I'd lightly inquire about our cattle drive's little mystery. "Weird thing about the cinch straps, huh?"

Lucky shrugged. His smile faded, and he stared straight ahead. "Nothing weird about it. Someone cut 'em."

"Any idea who?" I asked.

Lucky looked as if he was about to reply and then tightened his lips. After a moment, he shook his head. "Nope."

"Anyone who might have a grudge against Wally?" I asked.

"Not that I know of," he replied.

Lucky changed the subject by pointing past me. "Looks like Sarah found a few."

Sarah rode behind three cows. A large brown-and-white one raised its head and bellowed deeply. Ahead of us, the calf perked up its ears and answered with a bawl of its own. It broke into a run, cutting over to the large cow, who was obviously its mother.

"Help Sarah get those back to the herd," Lucky instructed. "I'm going to do a head count."

Lucky rode ahead as I followed the calf toward Sarah's group. When mother and calf were reunited, I steered Harvey to trot beside Sarah.

"I'm hoping that's all of them," she said with a smile. "So, how do you like your first day?"

"Interesting, to say the least," I replied. "But Harvey did all the work." I told her about his prowess herding the small calf.

Sarah laughed. "Dusty didn't tell you Harvey was a cutting horse before now? I should've warned you about those guys."

"What do you mean?" I asked.

"They like to play pranks on the new ranch hands," she explained. "Looks like you got off pretty lightly, though."

"The cut cinch straps weren't a prank, were they?" I asked.

Sarah shook her head, her expression darkening. "No, I think that was Mike and Tim."

"The ones who tried to steal your horse?" I asked.

"Yeah, that's them."

"Do they have a grudge against your father?"

"Well, he did get on them a couple of times," she explained. "For not doing their share of the work, things like that. It must be really bugging Lucky."

"Why is that?" I asked.

"Because he's the one who brought them in," she replied. "Apparently, they were friends of his from way back when."

"Lucky said he didn't know who cut the straps," I told her.

"He's probably embarrassed," said Sarah. "It doesn't look good for Lucky if he wants to be the top ranch hand."

"I thought you were the top hand," I said.

"I am now," she replied. "But someone has to take over when I go to college next year."

My eyes widened. "You're going to college already?"

Sarah rolled her eyes. "I'll be seventeen next month. Besides, since I'm homeschooled, I finished my high school classes early. Which is good, since I want to be a veterinarian. That means eight years of college, so I want to start early."

"A vet, huh? Cool."

By that point we had arrived back at the herd. Lucky gave us a thumbs-up from the opposite side.

"Looks like they're all accounted for," Sarah translated.

We rode over to the chuck wagon to find the rest of the crew lining up for lunch.

"You're just in time," said Wally. "Since we got waylaid

a bit, might as well have an early lunch. Tie up your horses and grab a tray. I'm afraid it's just going to be sandwiches for now, but I'll make up for that at dinner."

I didn't see my brother. "Where's Joe?"

"I'm here," came his voice from the back of the chuck wagon.

I climbed off my horse and walked over to peek in the back, where Joe sat tying knots in one of the cinch straps.

"I wanted to finish this first," he said. "Of course, everyone else repaired two or three each and this is my first and only one, but it's the thought that counts."

Yep, that was my stubborn brother.

"How do you feel?" I asked.

"Sore, but I'll live," he replied. He looked up from his work and grinned. "But who cares? We have a mystery to solve, bro!"

Yes, I had called it.

SCOUTING PARTY

6

JOE

I RAISED MY HANDS HIGH AS A LASSO WRAPPED around my body. "I surrender! Don't plug me, partner!"

Everyone laughed but Frank. After all, he was the one who had thrown the lasso. He was supposed to be aiming for a plastic cow's head that was attached to a wooden sawhorse. It was also a good ten feet away from me.

"Sorry," said Frank.

I slipped the rope off over my head as he reeled it in. "I thought I'd be safe way over here."

"You just released it a tad too soon," Sarah explained. "Here, let me show you again." She prepared her own lariat and then swung the open loop above her head. "Remember, keep rotating your wrist."

Sarah swung the rope two more times before letting it

fly. The looped lasso sailed over the fake calf nearby and encircled its head. Sarah pulled back, tightening the noose around its neck.

She removed the rope from the target and stepped back. "Okay, try again."

After lunch, while Lucky and the other hands tended the herd, Sarah had stayed behind to teach everyone how to throw a lasso. The Muellers had done a pretty good job their first time out. Mr. Jackson and I even nailed it the first time. Mr. Jackson had claimed beginner's luck, but I knew I had an unfair advantage: I'd been a lifeguard for three summers in a row. We'd practiced how to throw a lifeline to a drowning victim all the time. It wasn't a lasso, but it was close.

On the other hand, Frank hadn't been so skillful. Not only did he miss the target on the first two tries, but on the third, he lassoed his only brother. At first I thought it would kill him to be failing so miserably in front of such a pretty girl. But he didn't seem to mind—not even my gentle ribbing. Come to think of it, his clumsiness *was* getting him some extra attention. Could he be faking it to be teacher's pet? Nah. That seemed more like something I'd do.

Frank tried a fourth time, spinning the rope over his head and letting it fly. He didn't quite lasso the calf's head, but he came close. The rope landed on the back of the sawhorse.

"Much better," said Sarah.

"Thanks," Frank replied.

Wally closed a wooden panel on the chuck wagon and

sauntered over. "Sorry, you'll have to practice later, Frank. It's time to move 'em out."

Sarah patted Frank on the shoulder. "Tomorrow we'll try it on horseback."

"I'll be riding on the other side of the herd for that one," I said with a grin.

After a sore morning, I took some ibuprofen, which made my hip feel better enough to ride. Everyone climbed back onto their horses, Sarah directing us into position, and we got the herd moving. Wally and the chuck wagon brought up the rear, while the riders surrounded the herd and guided them across the open property.

The rest of the afternoon went more smoothly. We drove the herd across open pastures, through gaps in wooded areas, and over large hills. Soundtracks from some of my favorite westerns played in my mind as I rode my horse. I cycled through the themes from *Rio Bravo*, *Rio Lobo*, *Rio Grande*— all the John Wayne *Rio*s.

It would've felt cooler if my horse wasn't named Norman. I passed the time thinking of better horse names.

As I was debating between Apache and Buckshot, Frank rode up behind me. "How's it going, Tex?"

"Tex," I repeated. "That's a good one."

Frank gave me a puzzled look. "What's a good one?"

"Never mind." I shook my head. "Is this cool, or what?"

"I'm getting used to it," Frank replied. "I wouldn't choose this for a career, but it's fun for a weekend."

I thumped the brim of my cowboy hat. "I've always wanted to be a cowboy."

"My brother the dreamer," Frank said. "You know, if we were sentenced to a weekend at space camp, you'd say that you'd always wanted to be an astronaut."

I smiled and shrugged. "What can I say? It's good to keep your options open."

Frank glanced across the herd at Sarah. "I did want to get to know Sarah better, though. That's been cool."

"And?" I prodded.

Frank shrugged. "She's great. But I'm not asking her out, if that's what you're digging for."

"Oh, yeah?" I asked. "Getting cold feet?"

"It's not that. I just don't think she has time for dating," he explained. He told me about her plans to attend college early to be a vet.

I glanced around to see if anyone was within earshot. "Wouldn't that leave Lucky as the new top ranch hand?"

Frank lowered his voice. "Are you thinking what I'm thinking?"

"I think so." I lowered my voice too.

Frank told me what Sarah had said about how Lucky had brought in Mike and Tim in the first place.

"If Lucky's working with them, then he could've been the one to cut the straps," I said.

Frank shook his head. "But I don't see why he'd want to do that if he wants to be top hand."

"Maybe so he can swoop in and save the day? Look like a hero?" I suggested. Then I shook my head. "No, that doesn't make sense either."

"Yeah, right now it's just guilt by association," Frank pointed out. "And whoever's to blame, the motive isn't clear."

"That's what I told Wally," I said. "He did ask us to help him figure it out if we could."

"So we're officially on the case?" Frank asked.

"Well, more like unofficially officially," I replied.

"I think we'll have plenty of time to think it over before we get to the Welch ranch," Frank said. "In the meantime, Sarah asked that I take your place here while you take Mr. Jackson's place at the head of the herd."

"Cool," I replied. "We'll chat more later."

I gave Norman a gentle kick, and he loped alongside the herd. The theme from Clint Eastwood's *A Fistful of Dollars* played in my head as I passed the bellowing cattle, and I couldn't help but smile.

When I reached the front of the herd, I pulled up alongside Sarah and Dusty.

"There you are!" said Dusty. "I thought we were going to have to send a search party."

"Ride up front with us for a while, Joe," Sarah said. "I want everyone to get to work different aspects of the drive."

I adjusted my hat. "So what do we do up here?"

"Lead the way, stay ahead of the herd, and don't get lost," replied Sarah.

"Sure beats riding drag." Dusty grinned and jutted a thumb over his shoulder. "Back there, the scenery never changes."

I knew that firsthand. Bringing up the rear on a cattle drive was fun at first, but Dusty was right. You spend your time looking at cow butts.

"Bigger cattle drives would send a rider up ahead to scout the land first," Sarah explained.

"That sounds like fun," I said. I envisioned myself the lone rider looking for trouble on the western plains. "Want me to go?"

Sarah laughed. "Sure, if you know the way to the ranch."

My face fell. "I don't."

"We don't usually send out a scout on the way back," Sarah explained. "We did when we drove the cattle to Bayport, to make sure the path was clear of any downed trees or other obstacles. But it was smooth sailing."

"All right." I sat taller in the saddle. "But next time I'm your guy."

Sarah laughed. "Tell you what . . . go ahead. Just beyond the hill, you'll come to a small, shallow creek. You should see a gap in the trees where we'll cross."

"Yes, ma'am." I tipped my hat and kicked Norman's sides. The horse broke into a trot and moved ahead of the herd. When we were far enough away, I gave him another gentle kick. He responded at once by breaking into a smooth gallop.

"This is what I'm talking about," I said as the theme to *The Magnificent Seven* blared in my brain.

I rode up the small hill and stopped at the top. A gradual slope spread out before me. It ended at a line of trees snaking through the open pasture. That had to be where the creek was. I spotted a small opening in the trees and urged Norman forward, steering him toward the gap.

As we approached, I heard a sound competing with the thump of Norman's hoofbeats. It sounded like white noise, like a fan blowing, the ocean surf, or . . . running water. When I closed in on the creek, I saw the source of the sound. The *small* creek Sarah mentioned—it looked more like a raging river.

WATER CROSSING

7

FRANK

WELL, THIS BEATS ALL I EVER SAW." Wally stood high in his stirrups to get a better look at the swollen creek. "It's never been this bad."

Joe had been the first to spot the unusually high creek. After he reported the news to Sarah, she had Dusty, Ned, and the guests keep the cattle on the other side of the hill. That left me, Joe, Sarah, and Lucky to check out the creek firsthand. Even Wally had saddled a horse and joined us. Now, we all sat atop our horses looking at what was supposed to be a small creek. Except it looked like a wild, uncontrolled river. Water swept past us, forming little rapids and whitecaps.

"It hasn't rained lately," said Sarah. "So it can't be the result of flooding. Maybe the dam broke."

"I don't see how," said Lucky. "I swung by Rogers's lake when I scouted the trail on the way up to Bayport. Everything looked fine then."

Sarah turned to Joe and me. "We're at the back of Earl Rogers's ranch. He has a huge lake, but this creek is usually just the runoff from when it rains."

"So, I take it that this isn't normal?" I asked.

"Not even close," Sarah replied.

"We could take the herd off property," Lucky suggested. "Drive them onto County Road 4240 and use the bridge to cross."

Wally rubbed the back of his neck. "That would put us more than half a day behind. We'd have to spend another night out. Put us at the ranch midday on Monday."

"I don't mind missing Mr. Wilkins's calculus class," said Joe.

Joe wasn't kidding. Even though he was a pretty good student, I was the math nerd of the family. Besides, I could tell he was having way too much fun out here. I was sure that any amount of extra homework and makeup tests would be worth it if he could spend more time on the cattle drive.

"Sarah, check the crossing," Wally instructed. "See what we're dealing with."

Sarah turned Hondo and galloped down to the creek. She pulled him to a stop at the water's edge, then nudged him in. The water swirled around the horse's legs as he carefully moved farther in. We all watched with anticipation as he trod deeper; I realized that I was holding my breath. I exhaled just as Hondo reached the halfway point. The water churned violently around his belly.

Sarah gave Hondo another kick, and he trotted the rest of the way. Water splashed high around her as he reached the other side.

"Well, that's good news," said Wally. "It's moving fast, but it shouldn't reach much higher than the wagon's bottom. I think we can make it."

"You sure, boss?" asked Lucky. "The bridge would be safest."

"I think it's scarier than it looks," said Wally. "We should be fine." He smiled at Joe. "And I don't want to ever stand in the way of a young boy's fine education."

Joe sighed. "Thanks for that."

Wally waved Sarah back; she made the return crossing much faster. Hondo's hooves splashed water everywhere. She galloped up to us and pulled to a stop.

"We're going for it," Wally announced. "Lucky, you rope Buford and tie him to the back of the wagon. We'll cross first."

"Excuse me," I said. "But who's Buford?"

"That's our bull," Sarah answered. "With him leading the way, the rest of the herd will be more likely to follow."

"That's right," agreed Wally. "Lucky, I want you and our guests riding drag, driving them forward." He pointed to Joe and me. "I want the Hardys on one side and Ned and Dusty on the other. Sarah, round up any strays."

With our marching orders given, everyone rode back to the herd. Just as instructed, Lucky tossed a lasso around the horns of a big red bull. I hadn't noticed him before, but he was quite different from the rest of the cattle. Bulging muscles stretched his hide; he looked as if he could easily pull away from Lucky and his horse. However, the bull obediently followed as Lucky led him to the wagon. Once he was tied, Wally got the wagon going with the big bull in tow.

With the riders surrounding them, the cattle followed the wagon down the hill. Wally shook the reins and urged his mules into the wide creek. Buford seemed a little reluctant to step into the swift water, but he was no match for the large mules pulling the wagon. Soon, both wagon and bull were up to their bellies in water. Buford kept his nose up the rest of the way as they safely crossed.

With us riders on each side, the cattle soon followed, bellowing the whole way. I had removed a coiled lariat from my saddle and waved it to keep them moving. I saw Joe doing the same. Of course, he had a crazy grin on his face the entire time.

I was the first to reach the creek and was about to cross when Sarah stopped me.

"Hold right here," she ordered. "We'll make sure all the cattle cross before we join them."

I sat atop Harvey and watched the cattle trudge through the wide creek. My horse's ears pricked up as one of the cows tried to cut past us and run along the bank. Before I could react, Harvey's training kicked in. He immediately sidestepped, blocking the cow's path. The possible runaway thought better of her escape plan and turned to join the others as they crossed the creek.

Soon, I saw the back of the herd stream down the hill. Lucky, Mr. Jackson, and the Muellers waved their hats and lariats, driving them forward. The herd was almost completely through.

A blur of red and white caught my eye. It was the little calf we had chased earlier. It bawled as it zigzagged through the cattle. Its mother must've been somewhere near the front of the herd.

"I forgot about him," Sarah said as she opened a loop on her lariat. "He's too small to wade across. Let's see if I can rope him before he hits the water."

I didn't see how she could. The calf was winding a path through the much taller cows, rendering him barely visible. Sarah had shown she was good with a rope, but no one was that good.

Hondo trotted closer to the herd as Sarah swung her lasso over her head. The calf ran out for a moment, then, before she could let her lariat fly, ducked back into the herd. She moved her horse closer, but by that point the calf had already reached the water.

"Keep an eye out," she said. "I don't know if he'll be a good swimmer."

I moved Harvey closer to the bank as Sarah and I watched the little calf wade out with the rest of the cattle. It was so short, it was swimming while the rest of the cattle were up to their shoulders, wading.

With a loud cry, the calf hit the swift center of the creek and was swept downstream.

Sarah shook her head. "I knew it." She turned her horse and trotted along the bank. "Stand in the center of the creek," she ordered. "Make sure none of them follow him."

"Got it," I replied, and kicked Harvey forward. Splashes of cold water shot up my back as the horse trotted in past his knees. Once we were in the center of the stream, I turned Harvey to face the cattle. None of them seemed interested in following the little calf. They kept right on crossing the rapids toward the bank on the other side.

Hondo was galloping now as Sarah tried to outpace the little calf being swept through the churning water. Its bellow was cut off with a gurgle as its head dipped under the surface.

I should have been paying closer attention to the job at hand. Harvey shifted under me, and I turned back to see one of the cows trying to get past him. The horse sidestepped so fast that the cow didn't have a chance.

Startled, I pulled back on the reins by mistake. Harvey reared, and I felt myself slipping backward.

"Whoa, boy," I said, reaching for the saddle horn.

But my hand swiped through air. My arms flailed as I tumbled out of the saddle and splashed into the cold stream. I tried to call for help but got a mouthful of water instead. The current dragged me downstream away from the others.

MAVERICKS 8

JOE

ONE MINUTE FRANK WAS SITTING ON his horse in the middle of the churning water. The cattle were behaving and the crossing seemed to be going smoothly. When I looked up again, Frank's horse was still in the creek, but my brother was gone.

"Frank!" I shouted. I kicked Norman toward the water, but my brother was nowhere to be seen.

Norman plowed into the spot where I'd last seen Frank. I searched the stream and finally saw him being swept away. I knew my brother was a good swimmer. But between the swift water and his heavy cowboy boots, I wasn't going to take any chances.

I kicked Norman's sides, and he crossed the creek along with the cattle. I didn't think running downstream was an option. It would be too slow having Norman trudge through the deep water, or worse, I could end up like Frank. I had a better chance running along the shore.

I urged Norman faster as he galloped beside the rapids, and I kept my eye on my floating brother as he bobbed along. I lost sight of him behind the thick trees lining the creek but picked him up again as we passed a clearing.

"Come on, Norman." I kicked the horse's sides again, and he gained speed. I had to get ahead of Frank. I also had to find another opening in the tree line.

Finally I saw what I needed up ahead—a big gap in the trees. Norman and I raced toward it. When we arrived, I pulled the reins, jerking him to a stop.

The sides of the creek were so steep that there was no way I could've grabbed Frank as he passed. I had to do things the cowboy way. I opened a loop in my lasso and swung it over my head.

Norman paced nervously. "Steady, boy," I said, spinning the lasso faster.

Then Frank swept by. He reached out and grabbed a jutting log to catch himself but only slowed for a second before the wood broke away in his hand.

"I got ya, bro," I said to myself. "I hope."

As Frank neared, we locked eyes. He raised a hand, and I let my lasso fly. Unfortunately, the rope sailed in front of him, missing him completely. My lariat's loop unwound and floated ahead of him. I didn't have time for another shot, so I'd have to pull in the rope, gallop ahead of him, and hope to find another clearing.

But just before I began to reel it in, Frank swam forward and snagged the rope.

I laughed. "That's my brother!"

I wrapped the end of the rope around my saddle horn and steered Norman away from the creek. We slowly pulled Frank to shore. The pull against the current brought Frank's head underwater, but his hands held firm on my lariat. He was almost to the shore.

"Come on, Normy." I nudged the horse again. "Almost there."

When my brother was in shallow water, he stumbled to his feet. He coughed as he used the line to pull himself closer to the embankment. I walked Norman back to him, reeling in the rope as we went.

"You just had to go for a swim, huh?" I asked.

Frank trudged toward the steep bank. "Not really," he replied.

I kept the rope tight while Frank climbed the steep bank. He sat on the ground, took off one of his boots, then turned it over. Water poured out.

"Well, that was embarrassing," he said.

"I get it," I said. "You just didn't want me to feel bad for falling off a horse."

Frank shook his head as he emptied his other boot. "That's what brothers are for."

I coiled my lasso and helped Frank onto Norman's back. We rode double on our way back to the others.

As we came around the bend, we saw that the entire herd had crossed the churning creek. Lucky spotted us and rode out to meet us with Harvey in tow.

"Don't you boys know the number one rule of horseback riding?" he asked. "Always keep the horse between you and the ground."

Frank slid off the back of Norman. "I'll try to keep that in mind from now on." He looked up at me. "Thanks for the ride. And the save."

I tipped my hat in his direction. "All in a day's work."

Frank rolled his eyes and climbed back on Harvey. We quickly joined the rest of the cattle drive. Sarah splashed across the creek atop Hondo with a small brown-and-white calf draped over the saddle in front of her. She climbed down and brought the baby cow with her. After she set it on the ground, it bounded into the herd.

"How did it go?" she asked Lucky. "Did any get away from us?"

"They all made it across," Lucky replied. "I'm going to untie Buford so we can get going again." He grinned at Frank. "I'll let Frank fill you in on the rest." He trotted toward the chuck wagon.

Sarah gave Frank a concerned look. "I saw you go down!

By the time I got this little guy"—she nodded at the calf—"your brother had already fished you out."

Frank's face reddened with embarrassment. I couldn't let my brother go down like that.

"Frank and Harvey kept one of the cows from chasing down the calf," I said. "It was actually quite heroic," I added.

"The trouble is, Harvey zigged and I zagged," Frank finished. "Good thing Joe caught up to me and threw me a line."

My brother was too honest. He just couldn't leave the PR to me, could he?

Sarah smiled at Frank. "Don't worry. I can't even count how many times I've fallen off or been bucked off a horse. You'll get the hang of it."

"It's been quite an experience." Frank nodded in my direction. "But it's my brother here who seems to be a natural."

"Says the guy who always moans when I suggest a spaghetti western marathon," I said. "See, watching all those old movies paid off."

Sarah laughed. "Frank, why don't you ride up to the chuck wagon and change into some dry clothes. I'm sure my dad's ready to move them out anytime now."

"Thanks," said Frank. He turned Harvey and trotted toward the others.

"You up for another scouting mission?" asked Sarah.

I beamed. "You bet."

I helped the other riders get the herd moving again before peeling away from the group. Sarah had asked me to follow the creek up a couple of miles to the lake to check on the dam. If it had broken, as she suspected, then they'd have to let Earl Rogers know. Luckily, there was no way I could get lost. I just had to follow the creek, go through a couple of gates, and I'd run into the lake. After I checked it out, I just had to follow the creek back to the crossing and then follow the trail back to the herd. According to Sarah, I didn't need to be an expert tracker to follow their trail. Between the wagon ruts and the hoofprints, I couldn't miss it.

I stood in the stirrups as Norman galloped across the field. Blaring horns and beating drums played in my mind as I rode.

I passed through a couple of nearby gates, as expected, and continued to follow the creek as it snaked through the open fields. Sometimes I had to cut through some wooded outcrops, but the loud creek was easy to find again. I kept it on my right as I rode.

After about an hour, I could tell I was nearing my destination. The field ahead rose into a gradual incline. The large slope was the side of the earthen dam. I leaned forward in the saddle as Norman climbed up the side.

At the top, a beautiful lake spread out before me. It wasn't as big as some of the lakes around Bayport, but it was way too big to be called a pond. The opposite bank was dotted with large trees. On my side of the lake, the raised dam had been built wide enough that a vehicle could drive along the top without a problem.

I nudged Norman forward along the earthen dam. The spillway turned out to be nothing more than a large corrugated pipe jutting out of the side of the slope. If there was a lot of rain, the extra water would spill through the pipe and into the creek below. This controlled release would keep the earth dam from eroding over time. The rush of water grew louder as we approached, but no water spewed from the pipe. Instead water rushed out of a huge gash in the ground next to the large pipe.

I climbed off my horse for a closer look. I saw tracks, two of them, crisscrossing in front of the breach. They were wide, with thick lines crossing them like the timbers of train tracks; they looked like they were made by a bulldozer. As I inched closer to the gap in the dam, careful not to fall in, I saw that long tooth marks gouged the sides of the breach.

Over the years, mysteries have taken my brother and me to many different places. So I had investigated enough construction sites to guess that a person had dug this trench with some sort of backhoe—a tractor with a bucket on the end of a long mechanical arm. They were used to dig large holes very quickly. Some of them even ran on treads like those of a bulldozer or a tank.

There was no doubt about it. Someone had sabotaged the dam on purpose. Just one more piece of evidence that someone had it in for this cattle drive. The trouble was, we still didn't know why.

Or what they would try next.

IN CAHOOTS 9

FRANK

WALLY HAD HELD UP THE CATTLE drive just long enough for me to change in the back of the chuck wagon. I was thankful. It was hard enough pulling off wet clothes in the cramped space; I could only imagine how hard it would have been if the thing had been bouncing around as it moved down the trail. I tried to be as quick as possible, not wanting to hold everyone up even more than I already had.

When I was done, I climbed back onto Harvey and rode over to meet Sarah. My saddle was still wet, but it would have to dry along the way.

"You ride drag along with the Muellers," she instructed,

"and keep an eye out for Joe. He should catch up with us in a couple of hours."

"What do you mean?" I asked.

Sarah explained Joe's scouting mission. Then she rode off to get the rest of the team. Normally, I would've been worried about my brother riding alone. But with the way he had been handling himself this entire time, I wasn't. If Joe could ever live without the comforts of Bayport's shops, restaurants, and hangouts, he would make a fine cowboy.

We continued our long trek back to the ranch. As we moved away from the creek, the land became less lush and more scrubby. This helped move the cattle along, since there wasn't much on which they could stop and graze. Unfortunately, it showed me just how much of a drag riding drag could be. The Muellers and I rode in a cloud of dust kicked up by the shambling herd.

I wrapped the reins around my saddle horn so I could have both hands free. Luckily, I had thought to grab a fresh bandanna after I had changed. "Time for the bandit look," I told them as I wrapped the cloth over my mouth and nose and tied the ends behind my head.

"Oh yes," said Mrs. Mueller. "I forgot." She pulled up her bandanna to cover her nose.

Mr. Mueller did the same. When he was finished, he pointed his index finger at me, miming a six-shooter. "Stick 'em up!"

I jokingly raised both hands, and they laughed.

Riding drag on a cattle drive was mostly uneventful, which gave me plenty of time to think about our little cowboy mystery. Holding steady at the top of the suspect list were Mike and Tim, the disgruntled employees. After all, Joe and I had caught them in the act of trying to steal Sarah's horse. But I still didn't get why they would sabotage the cinch straps as well. Stealing a valuable horse was one thing, but why risk getting caught by taking the time to antagonize the boss one last time? It didn't really make sense.

Sarah rode by and offered to rotate us to other parts of the cattle drive. The Muellers jumped at the chance to leave the dusty drag position. I opted to stay behind and wait for Joe's return.

We drove the herd for a couple more hours before Wally called a halt for the day. The sun was low in the sky, and Joe had yet to return. Luckily, there was plenty of work to keep my mind occupied. We unsaddled our horses and tied them to the picket built by Ned and Dusty—two tall cedar stakes driven into the ground, with a rope running between them. After that, Sarah showed us how to wipe the sweat from our horses, check their hooves for loose horseshoes, and brush them down.

Then it was time to gather firewood. At least that was something I knew how to do. Joe and I had gone camping plenty of times.

I was just inside the edge of thick forest, looking for deadwood, when I heard galloping hooves. I stepped out to see Joe ride into the camp. I grabbed a couple more sticks before heading to meet him. He'd dismounted and was walking Norman around the camp.

"You taking your horse for a walk?" I fell into step behind him, and Norman followed us. His chest and sides were lathered with sweat.

"Sarah says Norman has to cool down before I tie him up with the others," he replied. "We had to run just to catch up with you before sundown."

"What did you find out?" I asked.

"Someone vandalized the dam," Joe replied. He explained how he had spotted the signs that a backhoe had cut a big hole in the side of the earthen dam.

"You told Wally and Sarah?" I asked.

"Yeah, and they weren't happy," replied Joe.

I tightened my lips. "More sabotage."

"You got it," agreed Joe.

"That seems like a lot of trouble for a couple of disgruntled employees," I said. "Were they trying to ruin the cattle drive?"

"Ruin it?" Joe asked. "With a big water crossing? That was actually kind of cool."

I raised my hand. "Hello? I wasn't planning on going for a swim today, you know."

Joe nodded. "So their big plan was to get Frank Hardy wet!"

I ignored my brother. "Well, they had to have known the herd could still cross the creek, even if it was swollen."

"Or that there was an alternate route available," Joe added. "Lucky had suggested that we take the herd onto another road to bypass the creek altogether."

I stopped walking. "Remember that he also mentioned that he had ridden by the lake on the way down. He said it was perfectly fine then. What if he sabotaged the dam?"

Joe stopped beside me and shook his head. "No way, bro. The damage was done with some heavy machinery, which was nowhere to be found. I don't think he could fit a backhoe into his saddlebags."

"But he could've had help," I suggested. "And the detour was his idea. What if his real plan was to get the herd somewhere else?"

"What? Like a trap?" Joe began to lead Norman again. "What good would that do? Try to steal Hondo again?"

"I don't know," I admitted.

I helped Joe unsaddle his horse and brush him down. By the time we joined everyone else, the campfire was roaring and dinner was being served. Wally grilled steaks and served them with a side of beans. There was also bread that had been baked in the ranch's brick oven. Everything was delicious.

During dinner, Joe and I kept our half-formed theories and suspect list to ourselves. There was no sense in pointing fingers at the moment, and we still had another half day's ride to the ranch.

Honestly, our suspect list wasn't very long. I didn't think

Wally and Sarah would do anything to spoil the cattle drive. The three paying guests, the Muellers and Mr. Jackson, all had less riding experience than Joe and me. I doubted they even knew what a cinch strap was before yesterday.

That left the three ranch hands. Dusty and Ned had seemed all right. They worked hard and were great at teaching everyone what to do. But they weren't the ones who had ridden to the dam on the drive in.

That was Lucky.

Lucky seemed to be the best cowboy of the bunch. He was a good leader and would probably make an excellent top ranch hand when Sarah went off to college. However, being friends with the failed horse thieves did put him at the top of our list—that along with his previous visit to the dam.

After dinner, everyone sat around the campfire, replaying the day's events and listening to stories. Then Ned surprised us by pulling a guitar from the back of the wagon and singing some cowboy songs. Dusty accompanied him on an old, dented harmonica, and Mrs. Mueller turned out to have a very nice singing voice. They had all of us clapping along.

Later, when I stretched out on my bedroll and propped my head on my saddle, I realized that Ned had been right. I was so beat from the day's work that the thin blanket on the hard ground felt like heaven. I gazed up at the night sky, marveling at the view. Away from the city, the dark sky was alive with twinkling stars. The thin arm of the Milky Way reminded me of the creek we'd crossed earlier. I was about to whisper as much to Joe, but I heard him lightly snoring beside me. My eyes drifted shut as I felt myself falling into much-needed sleep.

Just as I was slipping into a dream of riding Harvey across the open plains, I was nudged awake.

"Frank," a voice whispered.

I opened my eyes to see Ned kneeling over me. The coals from the dying campfire illuminated his face in dim, amber light.

"What's wrong?" I asked. My first thoughts were of another act of sabotage.

The cowhand grinned. "Secret mission."

I sat up and snatched my boots while Dusty roused Joe.

Keeping quiet, my brother and I followed Ned and Dusty away from the others. I caught Joe's eye, but he merely shrugged. Once we were far enough away from everyone, the ranch hands switched on dim flashlights. They turned them to illuminate their faces.

"What's going on, guys?" Joe asked.

Dusty shifted the toothpick between his lips. Did he sleep with that thing? "Greenhorn initiation," he said solemnly.

Ned nodded. "Yep. All new ranch hands go through it."

I held up my hands. "Look, guys. We're just here for the weekend."

"Doesn't matter," said Dusty. "You're cowhand enough."

I glanced at Joe. His eyes were gleaming—probably from the excitement of being called a cowhand.

Ned must have read my look of unease. "Don't worry. It's nothing bad."

Dusty clapped a hand on my shoulder and led me toward the quiet cattle herd. "Just a little cow tippin'."

I stopped. "Cow tipping?" I asked. "That's not real."

Ned and Dusty exchanged looks of shock. "Sure, it's real," said Ned. "Not much to do living out in the country. Cow tippin' is quite the pastime."

I had read about cow tipping, of course. The object was to sneak up on a sleeping cow and tip it over. Cows were supposed to sleep standing up, so the animal would just fall over before waking.

I'd also heard that it was nothing but an urban legend.

"I didn't think cows even slept standing up," I said. To prove my point, I gestured at a few of the nearest cows. The dark shapes were lying in the grass, their four legs tucked beneath them. Some were motionless; others quietly chewed.

Dusty pulled out his toothpick and pointed it at me. "Shows what you know, city slicker. Not *all* cows sleep standing up. Those that do, you can tip."

"I'm in," Joe whispered. "As long as it doesn't hurt them."

"Not at all," replied Ned. He waved for us to follow. "Come on." Keeping his flashlight beam low, he led us deeper into the herd.

I caught up to Joe. "We're being punked, you know," I whispered. "It can't be real."

Joe shrugged. "Why not?"

I shook my head and followed my brother and our two guides as they snaked through the herd. Most of the cattle kept to the ground as we passed. Finally Ned and Dusty stopped ten feet away from a dark shape and switched off their flashlights.

"There she is," Ned whispered. "What did I tell you?"

I could make out the shape of a cow, silent and unmoving in the dim moonlight. I guess some of them did sleep standing up.

"That's your target," Dusty whispered.

I turned to Joe and gestured to the dark shape. "You first."

Ned shook his head. "No, no. It's gonna take two of you. And you'll need a good running start from here. Remember, these cows weigh over a thousand pounds."

Dusty handed me his flashlight. "And hold on to this. You're going to want to see her expression when she goes down. Just keep it off until you're done."

"You don't want to wake her before you can tip her," added Ned.

"You sure this doesn't hurt them?" Joe asked again.

"Oh no," Ned replied. "Just a rude awakening."

"You'll love it," Dusty added.

Joe looked at me and I shrugged. I still didn't quite believe it, but I was exhausted. If waking up a cow would let *me* go back to sleep, I wanted to get it over with.

"On three," Joe whispered. "One . . . two . . . three."

We charged the sleeping cow, closing the ten feet in no

time and slamming into the huge animal. It was like hitting a cowhide-covered brick wall. We hit the ground beside her. The beast didn't tip, but did stir. I switched on the flashlight just as her head swung around to look at us. That's when I realized two things. One: cow tipping is not real. And two: this wasn't a cow, it was a bull. He glared at us with big eyes set beneath even bigger horns.

"Bull!" I shouted, scrambling backward.

"Oh, man!" said Joe as he clambered to his feet.

We both made it to our feet only to slam into each other and fall back to the ground. The flashlight beam flared wildly across the animal looming over us.

At once, Ned and Dusty were between us and the bull. At first I thought they were trying to save us. Instead they were doubled over with laughter.

Still on the ground, I looked at my brother. "What did I tell you?"

Ned helped us to our feet while Dusty patted the bull on his meaty shoulder.

"You were right, Frank. Cow tipping is a myth," confirmed Ned.

"And another myth is that all bulls are mean," Dusty added. He scratched the bull's forehead. The animal snorted and closed his eyes, seeming to enjoy the attention. "Old Buford here wouldn't hurt a fly."

CATTLE RUSTLERS

10

JOE

EVERY SPRING, I'D GET MY TEN-SPEED out of the garage for the first time since winter. I would air up the tires, oil the chains, and all that. Then, if it was a nice day, I would go for a nice long bike ride.

Then there was the *next* day, when I'd wake up sore because I hadn't sat on that tiny seat all winter long. It would be . . . hard to sit down.

Well, that's how I felt in the morning when I climbed into the saddle. My butt was sore from riding the previous day. At least I thought it was from riding; it might have been from landing on it when Frank and I had slammed into that bull. And speaking of sore . . . the hip I'd fallen on after being thrown off Norman yesterday? Ouch.

We'd started the day with a big breakfast (during which Ned and Dusty regaled the others with tales of the Hardy brothers' "initiation"), and then everyone saddled up and moved out the herd.

It was a clear day and the cattle were going with the program, for the most part. Only once did I have to chase down a young heifer that had strayed too far from the herd. When she saw me galloping toward her, she quickly cut back to the others. If it had been the day before, I would have relished the thought of having a bit more of a chase, maybe even roping the stray cow. But the pain I felt every time I bounced in the seat made me glad the cow wasn't so bold.

Sarah and Lucky had everyone rotate around the herd, same as the day before. Because we worked different positions, I didn't see much of Frank. When I did see him, he was with Sarah. For someone who said he wasn't so interested, Frank sure was spending a lot of time with her.

It wasn't long before I found myself riding drag again. We had crossed to another ranch, and the pasture was more lush than the last one. But the herd still kicked up enough dust that I had to wear a bandanna over my mouth and nose. Lucky joined me behind the herd. He pulled up his bandanna too. I decided to take the chance to interrogate our main suspect.

"So how is the drive going overall?" I asked.

"Good," he replied. "We should reach the main ranch before sundown. All the pranks have put us a bit behind schedule."

I adjusted my bandanna. "Any other obstacles to worry about?"

Lucky cocked his head at me. "What do you mean?"

"You know, swollen water crossings, things like that," I explained.

The cowhand shook his head. "Nope. Just a couple more gates to get through." He pointed ahead of the herd. "We should be coming up to Wilson's spread in about a mile."

I felt a pang of disappointment. I was kind of sorry to see it end. Getting to sleep in my own bed tonight meant calculus tomorrow.

I shook those thoughts from my mind; I had to stay on topic.

"So, what was up with that dam?" I asked. "Any ideas?"

Lucky shrugged. Since his face was covered, I couldn't read his expression. "Could've been that Rogers was working on it and somehow botched the job."

If that were the case, and it was a botched job, why would someone get rid of the equipment that made the hole in the first place? "So you don't think it was done on purpose?" I asked.

"I don't see what good that would do," Lucky replied. "From what you described, it's going to have to be fixed; otherwise the hole is going to get bigger."

"What about those guys who tried to steal Hondo?" I asked, deciding on the direct approach. "Wally thinks they might've cut the cinch straps too."

Lucky didn't reply for a long time. For a moment, I thought maybe I had blown the interrogation. If I were a detective on a cop show, this would be the part where the suspect asks for a lawyer.

"Yeah, I feel rotten about that," he finally said. "I'm the one who brought those boys on, so I feel somewhat responsible." He shook his head. "I still don't know why they would do such a thing. Sure, Wally came down on them hard a couple of times, but they had it coming. They were always slacking off." Lucky leaned back in the saddle. "Heck, I know they needed the work, so I don't see why they would throw that away."

I didn't reply, a tactic Frank and I had learned from our dad. Sometimes, given the chance, suspects will continue speaking just to fill an uneasy silence. Lucky didn't seem like a suspect, though. I couldn't read his expression, but he sounded genuinely remorseful. I rode quietly and watched the herd pass over the hill in front of us.

"Yeah, they probably cut the straps outta meanness," he continued. "But I don't see why they would mess with that dam. The high water didn't stop us. And even if it did, there was still a way around it."

I didn't have any other questions, so we rode in silence for a while. Well, silence in the fact that we quit talking. As usual, the cattle had plenty to say. They continued the sporadic moos they had been making throughout the entire trip.

Once we'd followed the herd down the opposite hillside, I could just make out the fence line in the distance. Of course, I couldn't see the barbed wire, but I saw rows of fence posts dotting the lower horizon.

As we reached the bottom of the hill, a strange sound competed with the bawling cattle and the hoofbeats. It seemed out of place here in the country but was a familiar sound to a city slicker like myself—the tinny hum of a motor. I looked around but couldn't spot the source.

"You hear that?" I asked Lucky.

The cowhand was already scanning the horizon. "Yeah. Sounds like an ATV or something. Some ranchers ride them instead of horses."

The sound grew louder and deeper. My ear picked out more than one motor approaching.

Lucky and I both spun in our saddles as a dirt bike crested the hill. Its helmeted rider leaned forward, seeming to aim his bike right at us.

"Whoa, boy," I told Norman as he shuffled nervously.

Three more dirt bikes followed. Their throttles whined louder as they turned toward the herd.

Lucky took off his hat and waved it over his head. "Hey! Stay back!"

The riders ignored him and raced closer, chasing the herd. The cattle bellowed and began to flee. The riders raced by us, chasing the herd.

"Hey!" I shouted.

I leaned forward as Norman reared into the air. It was all I could do to stay in the saddle. If I had so much trouble, there was no telling how the other riders would react with a hundred head of terrified cattle running at them.

"Stampede!" Lucky screamed. He kicked his horse and chased after the dirt bikes.

I got Norman under control and galloped after Lucky.

SPOOKED 11

FRANK

ARAH AND I WERE RIDING IN FRONT OF the herd, with the chuck wagon a hundred feet in front of us, when the sound of thunder filled the air. But there wasn't a cloud in the sky.

Sarah was the first to turn in her saddle. Her eyes widened. "Oh no."

I looked back to see a cloud of dust as the herd began galloping. A wave of motion rippled through the cattle as they broke into a run. The cows directly behind Sarah and me looked back anxiously. The entire herd would be upon us in no time.

Sarah cupped a hand to her mouth. "Clear out of the way! Stampede!"

Wally quickly glanced over his shoulder before snapping

the long reins against the backs of his mule team. They broke into a run and angled away from the approaching mass of cattle.

I pulled alongside Sarah. "What scared them?"

She pointed to distant figures on dirt bikes. "What are they doing?" she asked.

The riders looked out of place in our western tableau. I hadn't heard them over the roar of the thumping hooves, but now I could make out the sound of their buzzing motors. There were four of them bearing down on the herd. As they drew near, they swerved closer and closer to the terrified cattle. The riders seemed to move with purpose; they knew exactly what they were doing.

Furious, I kicked Harvey into a run. "Yah!" I shouted. I steered him toward the two riders teasing the west side of the stampeding cattle. I stood in the stirrups as Harvey poured on the speed. With the riders zipping in my direction, the gap between us closed quickly.

The second rider peeled away as I approached, speeding away from the stampede and into the pasture. I kicked Harvey again as I steered toward the rider in front, who was closing in fast.

I don't know if I had gotten used to being in the saddle or if I was just angry seeing the cows so frightened. Either way, I found myself in a game of chicken with a guy on a dirt bike. And I was on a horse. Not the smartest move.

My rational mind finally kicked in as I pushed down on

the stirrups and leaned back, ready to pull Harvey to a stop. In this case, I didn't mind being the chicken.

I guess the dirt biker had the same idea. He jerked his handlebars and skidded to a stop. However, his momentum was too great. A wave of sod erupted in front of him as his dirt bike plowed to a stop, and he fell off, the bike landing partly on top of him.

There was no way I could stop Harvey in time. And even if I had, I'd probably go flying off over his head. I jerked the reins to one side, trying to steer around the fallen biker. Harvey didn't obey. Instead he lowered his head and kept running. We were going to crash.

That was when I felt the strangest sensation. The ride atop the horse had been bumpy and rhythmic, but suddenly it was smooth. Then I felt a sense of weightlessness before I slammed back into the saddle. Harvey had jumped the downed rider!

After a few feet, I pulled Harvey to a stop and spun him around. The rider slid out from under his dirt bike, hopped back on, and revved the motor. I kicked Harvey forward as the rider peeled out, heading away from me, Harvey, and the stampede.

The last of the herd ran by as Lucky galloped up to me. "Good job, Frank," he said. "Now help Sarah and the others turn the herd. Joe and I will get the others."

"Turn the herd?" I asked.

"Yeah, turn 'em!" he repeated. "If they hit that barbed-wire fence, they'll get all kinds of cut up!"

GET A ROPE 12

HAD DONE FAIRLY WELL ROPING SARAH'S PRACTICE steer. Now I had to rope a moving target atop a galloping horse. I hoped my luck would hold.

Norman kept pace beside the dirt bike as it sped alongside the stampeding herd. I spun the lasso over my head, remembering to rotate my wrist just as Sarah had shown us. The terrified cattle bawled as they churned up the ground nearby. I tried to tune out the chaos of the stampede and concentrate on my target.

I released the lasso and watched it fly. Time seemed to slow as the wide loop sailed from my hand to the rider. For a moment, it seemed as if I had overshot the mark, the lasso flying in front of the helmeted man. Then he accelerated and drove right into the waiting loop. It tightened around his arms as he pulled away.

"Yeah!" I shouted in triumph.

I wrapped the other end of my rope around the saddle horn and pulled Norman to a stop. The rope tightened and jerked the rider off the dirt bike, slamming him to the ground.

Up ahead, a second dirt biker glanced over his shoulder, skidded to a stop, then spun around. He popped a wheelie as he accelerated toward me. I had taken care of one motorbike rustler with only one rope, but I had no idea what to do about the second guy.

Luckily, I wasn't alone. I heard loud hoofbeats behind me. Lucky galloped toward us, evening the odds.

My brief distraction was all the first rider needed. When I turned back, he had already slipped out of my lasso and was running toward the other rider. I quickly reeled in my rope, preparing for another throw.

Lucky galloped past me, his own rope in hand. He smacked his horse's rump to gain speed. I kicked Norman into a run and gave chase.

Ahead, the dirt bike had pulled to a stop and the downed rider climbed on behind the driver. The motorcycle popped another wheelie just as Lucky was upon them. Lucky's horse reared back in surprise, and mine came to a halt beside it.

"What are you doing, Lucky?" a voice asked. "Look out!"

Since both wore helmets with tinted faceplates, I couldn't tell which rider had spoken. But whoever it was knew Lucky.

The motorbike spun around, peeling out in the soft earth. A plume of dirt sprayed toward us, and both horses shied away. The two rustlers sped from the herd, the whine of the motor growing softer.

"Come on!" Lucky said as he kicked the sides of his horse. He sped alongside the stampede.

Urging Norman on, I raced to join him. We stayed in tight formation as we slowly outpaced the running cattle.

"They're going to turn the herd." Lucky pointed to the front of the panicked cattle. "That's where we come in."

"What do we do?" I asked.

"The only way to stop a stampede is to turn it into itself," he explained. "And I can't do it alone."

As we sped toward the front, I noticed what the others were doing. The chuck wagon, Mr. Jackson, and the Muellers stood to the right, away from the action. Up ahead, four riders moved up the line, to the right of the herd. That had to be Sarah, Ned, Dusty, and Frank. They waved hats and lariats, shooing the cattle away from that side. Slowly, the galloping mass of cattle changed course.

"Follow me!" Lucky ordered. He peeled to the left, veering away from the stampede. I directed Norman to follow.

We rode into the open pasture, away from the turmoil of the stampede. The thundering hooves grew softer behind us. When we were about fifty yards away, Lucky pulled his horse to a stop. I did the same. Lucky squinted as he scanned the front of the herd.

"What are we—" I began to ask.

Lucky held up a hand. I followed his gaze and watched the herd slowly arc to the left. The mass of cattle made a giant U-turn and began running right for us.

"Now it's our turn," Lucky said. "Yah!" He kicked his horse and rode straight toward the oncoming cattle.

"This is crazy!" I yelled as I followed his lead.

After their big turn, the cattle weren't running quite as fast, but I have to say, riding straight toward an advancing herd of cattle was daunting.

I followed Lucky as he approached the cattle. He pulled his horse to a stop and waved his lariat over his head. The lead cows turned sharply, running toward the tail end of the stampede. I pulled up alongside Lucky and did the same with my rope. The cattle slowed to a trot as they moved closer to their running herd members. The front of the herd pulled to a stop before colliding with the tail end of the herd. Like a ripple effect, the entire stampede halted.

We were back to being a bunch of riders surrounding a docile, albeit out-of-breath, herd of cattle.

BADLANDS 13

FRANK

NE OF THE GUYS CALLED HIM BY NAME," Joe told me. We rode side by side at the front of the herd.

"It was probably Mike or Tim," I said. "Of course they would know Lucky."

"Yeah, but you weren't there, bro." Joe glanced over his shoulder to see if anyone was around. "It almost seemed like the guy wondered why Lucky was interfering with their plans."

That put a different spin on things. "Did you ask Lucky about it?" I asked.

Joe shook his head. "I pretended like I didn't hear. Besides, we had the whole stopping-the-stampede thing to worry about."

"That was intense," I said.

"Yeah!" Joe's eyes gleamed. "I can't believe you jumped a dirt bike."

"A downed dirt bike," I corrected.

After the stampede fiasco, Wally had called a break for lunch. It was important to let the horses and cattle rest after their run. My adrenaline was still up from the stampede, so it had been hard to eat. Everyone else seemed to feel the same; there had been more talking than eating. The guests and cowhands had rehashed the exciting events from each of their perspectives. Lucky told everyone about how he saw me jump the dirt bike. I had given due credit to Harvey. After all, he had been the one jumping; I had been the one holding on for dear life.

Lucky hadn't mentioned the rustler calling his name, however. Wally had even blamed the event on—his term— "idiot kids" joyriding and spooking the cattle for a laugh. I remembered now that Lucky hadn't bothered to correct him and said as much to Joe.

"You're right," Joe said. "And I sure didn't want to bring it up in front of everybody, at least without telling you first."

"Think we should tell him now?" I asked.

Joe glanced over at the chuck wagon. Wally kept the mules driving parallel with the herd. "We still don't have any solid proof that Lucky's involved."

I sighed. "You're right." I spun in the saddle, trying to locate Sarah. I spotted her riding two positions back, on the left side of the herd. "Let me talk to Sarah first. You got this for a minute?"

Joe pointed to the path ahead. "Hard to get lost now."

The closer we traveled to the Welch ranch, the more obvious the trail became. Wally must have run many cattle drives near this point. Hoofprints and wagon ruts stretched across the pasture before us.

I turned Harvey and urged him back along the herd.

"Jumpin' Frank Hardy," Dusty said as I rode by.

I pulled up to Sarah and turned Harvey to walk beside her.

"You getting bored up there?" she asked.

"No, it's great being in front for a change," I said. "I just wanted to ask you something."

Sarah winked. "And here I thought you just missed my sparkling personality."

I blushed. I did enjoy talking to her. In fact, she was the main thing making this trip enjoyable. I was too shy (or stupid) to tell her that, though. "Uh, so what do you think those dirt bikers were up to?"

Sarah raised an eyebrow and smiled. "My father told me that the Hardy boys were trying to solve our little mystery."

"We may not be great cowboys," I started, and then corrected myself. "Well, *I* may not be a great cowboy. But as detectives, we're not too shabby."

"The dirt bikes . . ." She trailed off, then looked up in thought. "Well, they're probably just what my dad said," she replied. "Stupid kids, you know?"

"What if they weren't just kids?" I asked. "Could four guys on dirt bikes steal a whole herd?"

"Like *real* cattle rustlers?" she asked. "I don't think so. You know how hard it would be to run cattle with a loud, smelly dirt bike? And just four of them too." Her brow furrowed. "Why do you ask?"

"I—we think it was Mike and Tim again," I explained. "If not them, than at least someone Lucky knows." I reported what Joe had heard.

"Those dirty snakes." Sarah frowned. "Why won't they leave us alone?"

"What we don't understand is what they're trying to accomplish," I said. "If they couldn't steal the herd, then what?"

"I don't know." She shook her head. "To get back at my dad somehow."

"They're going through an awful lot of trouble just because your dad reprimanded them."

"Well, you chased them off easily enough," she said.

"Joe and I got lucky," I admitted. "But if we hadn't been here, between you and the other cowhands, they would've been chased off regardless."

"They did try to steal Hondo back in Bayport," she said.

"Yeah, and that kind of motive I understand." I pointed at Hondo. "He's a great horse and probably worth a lot of money. But if they were behind the cinches, maybe the dam, and now this . . . it all seems kind of . . . prankish."

She thought for a moment. "You're right. They didn't even go after Hondo when they stampeded the cattle."

"Do you think Lucky would know anything else about it?" I asked.

Sarah eyed me suspiciously. "What? Like he's involved somehow?"

I shrugged. "Joe said that one of the guys seemed surprised that Lucky helped chase them off. Almost like he had been in on it."

"Lucky's been with us for years." Her lips tightened. "He's the best ranch hand on the spread."

I raised both hands. "Hey, as a detective, I gotta look at all possibilities."

Sarah rolled her eyes. "Well, maybe you should save your detective work for the city." She pulled Hondo to a stop and spun him around. "Stay in this position," she ordered. "It's time to rotate anyway." Hondo broke into a gallop, and she rode to the back of the herd.

I sighed and glanced up at Joe. He cringed when I caught his eye; I guess he had seen her ride off angry. It didn't take any kind of brotherly telepathy for him to know that I had made Sarah Welch very mad.

SIDEWINDERS 14

JOE

FOR THE NEXT COUPLE OF HOURS, SARAH avoided the Hardy brothers like the plague. I only got to chat briefly with Frank during that time, but he confirmed my suspicions; Sarah wasn't at all happy about us accusing Lucky.

"Let me talk to her," I offered.

"No, just let it be," Frank said. "I think she's great, but she's about to go off to college. It's not like we can start dating or anything."

I nodded. "But what about the mystery? We're almost done with the drive, and we're still nowhere on the case. The Hardys have a reputation to uphold, you know?"

"Yeah, I've been racking my brain about that," he

admitted. "It seems backward. We think we know who's responsible, but we don't know the motive."

"We'll figure it out," I said. "I have complete and utter faith in our abilities." I goaded Norman into a trot. "Besides, if this detective thing doesn't work out, I'd make a pretty good cowboy."

Frank shook his head as I rode to the next position in the drive.

We continued the rotation until I found myself riding alongside Sarah at the front of the herd. We rode quietly for a while as she continued giving me the silent treatment. Finally I steered Norman closer to her.

Sarah held up a hand. "I don't want to hear it, Joe. Let's just get this herd home and be done."

I shook my head. "Okay, forget we said anything about Lucky. Let's talk about the cattle drive. Is there anything else we should watch out for?" I asked. "You think these guys will pull something else before we get to the ranch?"

Sarah seemed to ponder whether to respond. Finally she sighed. "I don't see how. We're almost there." She pointed ahead. "Once we crest this hill, we ride down to one more gate. After that, we're on the Double W proper. Another hour south and we're at the ranch house."

"No more possible obstacles?" I asked. "Any other way those guys can mess with us?"

Sarah thought for a moment. "Not that I can think of. But maybe I should scout ahead."

I sat up in the saddle. "Ooh! Send me in, Coach!" I wanted the chance to ride out alone again. The drive was almost over, and I had no idea when I'd get another opportunity like this.

"Well, I guess I should stay and help get the herd through the last gate," she said. "All right. You can't miss the way there."

"Got it!" I began to kick Norman, then stopped. "You know, Frank didn't mean to offend you. He just wants to help you and your dad." Before she could respond, I kicked Norman into a gallop.

I smiled. That's right. I still had my brother's back.

I rode over a large hill and spotted the fence below. I slowed Norman to a trot and kept my eyes open. I squinted, imagining that I was Clint Eastwood looking for trouble.

There was no mistaking the entrance to Wally Welch's ranch. The large metal gate was adorned with two giant *W*s. Everything was quiet as I scanned the pockets of trees on the other side of the fence. It was a good place for an ambush.

I opened the gate, led Norman through, and latched it shut behind me. Then I climbed back onto the horse and listened. All was quiet. I could just make out the sound of the cattle drive behind me.

I continued down the wide path through scattered trees and open pastures. Sarah had said it was an hour's ride to the main ranch house. She probably meant it was an hour going as slowly as the herd traveled. I kicked Norman into a gentle lope so I would get there sooner.

I grinned as I contemplated our weekend. Growing up in Bayport, I'd never had a chance to play cowboy. Learning to ride at summer camp didn't count. But here I was, riding a real horse on a real cattle drive. I got to experience a water crossing and a stampede, and I'd fought off cattle rustlers. Even if they were just dudes on dirt bikes, it was still exciting. Thanks to the pranksters, the cattle drive had lasted even longer.

Maybe that was it. What if delaying the cattle drive was the hidden motivation behind the sabotage? It was the only explanation that fit all the clues. What if the would-be horse thieves never intended to stop the cattle drive or steal anything? Every nefarious act had succeeded in only one thing: slowing us down. The cattle drive was supposed to be over before noon on Sunday. Now it was late afternoon. What if the true crime was happening right now at the ranch? What if Mike and Tim had just wanted to keep everyone away?

I kicked Norman's sides, and he broke into a full run. I had to get to the ranch and see if my hunch was correct.

I galloped across open pastures, over rolling hills, and around groves of trees, concentrating on keeping Norman on the path.

I crested a hill and pulled to a stop when I saw the WW homestead below. Nestled among large trees, the white farmhouse had a wide porch. A small chicken coop sat nearby, with chickens pecking inside a closed pen. Farther away, a long brown building must have been a bunkhouse for the ranch hands; it looked just like the ones in movies. And to top off the view, there was a red barn surrounded by wooden corrals and cattle pens.

I'd never been there before, so I wouldn't know if anything was out of place, but it all looked perfectly normal. Maybe I had rushed all the way there for nothing.

Just then I heard a sound from the west and spotted movement out of the corner of my eye. In the distance, two men on horseback galloped away. Nothing more than specks on the horizon, they rode up a small hill before disappearing from sight.

Was that Mike and Tim? Had they heard my loud approach and made a break for it?

I had almost decided to trail them when I spotted a thin tendril of smoke drifting up from the barn. Any western fan knows that barns don't have fireplaces or stoves; fire and hay don't mix. As the seconds ticked by, the smoke grew thicker.

"Oh no," I muttered.

I kicked Norman's sides once again, and we sped down the hill, toward the burning barn.

BUCKET BRIGADE

15

FRANK

"WELCOME TO THE DOUBLE W RANCH!" Wally said as we drove the last of the cattle through the gate. He stood in the chuck wagon as I closed the gate behind everyone. The riders gathered in front of the wagon as the cattle moved by.

Wally raised a hand. "Now, I know we're running late and we were supposed to end with a fine lunch down at the ranch house. But don't worry. We'll have a *dinner* instead before shuttling you back to Bayport. A nice barbecue." He tipped his hat back on his head. "We have about another hour to go, but as you can see, it's going to be an easy one." He pointed to the moving herd. They walked ahead of us down the wide path. They clearly knew the way and seemed eager to return home.

Wally continued, "I want to thank you all for a job well done. Even though we had a few hiccups along the way, I hope you had fun."

"Let's take 'em home!" Sarah shouted.

Wally got the wagon moving down the trail as we were given our assignments: Lucky and Mr. and Mrs. Mueller on one side, Ned and Mr. Jackson on the other side, and Dusty riding drag. I hadn't seen Joe in a while, so I assumed Sarah had him scout ahead before we hit the gate. He had told me how much fun he'd had scouting the dam. I was sure he was cramming in as much cowboy fun as possible before the weekend ended. I was surprised when Sarah finished the assignments by having me ride lead with her.

We rode a few paces ahead of the herd, keeping our horses at a trot since the cattle were moving faster.

"Look, I'm sorry I snapped at you," Sarah said. "Joe mentioned that you just had my best interests in mind."

I had told my brother not to say anything, but whatever he had said to Sarah seemed to have smoothed things out.

"He's right," I said. "We were just trying to figure out why these things were happening. It's hard to solve a mystery when you don't have a motive."

"I don't know much about solving mysteries," she admitted. "I just know Lucky wouldn't do anything to hurt the ranch or us."

"Fair enough," I replied. I still had my doubts about the cowhand, but there was no point in pushing it with Sarah.

"Maybe there isn't a motive," she suggested. "Maybe these really were just stupid pranks meant to get back at my dad."

"Well, getting back at your dad *would* be a motive," I said. "It just seems like a weak one for all the trouble these guys have gone through. That's what doesn't make sense to us."

"I see your point." She paused. "It's not very good revenge, if you ask me. All that stuff just slowed us down a little." She grinned. "And the stampede was exciting."

Lost in thought, I didn't reply. I was finally starting to put the pieces together. If Mike and Tim were behind everything, then they had probably accomplished what they had set out to accomplish. Everything they had done had put us behind schedule. The bigger question was: Why?

"Frank?" Sarah asked. "Earth to Frank."

We topped a small hill and began trotting down the other side. It was a good thing that Harvey knew the way home too. I had totally spaced out.

I blinked. "What? Oh, yeah."

But it was Sarah's turn to space out. She stared into the distance and didn't speak.

"Sarah?" I asked.

She held up a hand and shushed me, pulling Hondo to a stop. I did the same with Harvey. Things were much quieter with the wagon and shuffling herd behind us. A light breeze rustled the tall grass. Birds sang in the treetops. A lone bell rang in the distance.

"That's the ranch bell," Sarah explained.

"Is it Joe?" I asked.

"Maybe. I don't know. But that bell usually means trouble." She spun Hondo around and galloped back up the hill. I followed her as she stopped in front of the wagon. "Bell's ringing, Dad."

"You two check it out," Wally replied. "I'll send the others after you. Go, go!"

We galloped down the clear path that cut through the ranch. I did my best to hold on as Harvey kept pace with Hondo. When the rest of the cowhands caught up to us, it felt like we were in a posse chasing down bank robbers. Joe would've loved it. As for me, I kept a tight grip on the saddle horn, hoping I wouldn't fall off.

As we reached the top of the last hill, the WW ranch complex came into view. No one stopped to admire the sights, but I immediately saw why. A column of black smoke billowed from a big red barn.

"Joe," I said, my stomach tightening. I goaded Harvey to run faster.

Our group swarmed over the hill and sped to the ranch. I was relieved when I finally spotted Joe. My younger brother hurriedly led a wide-eyed horse out of the barn and into the nearby pens.

"Call 911?" I shouted. I regretted letting Wally confiscate our cell phones.

Sarah shook her head. "No time."

"Why hasn't the sprinkler system kicked in?" Lucky asked.

"I don't know," replied Sarah. We were closing in on the barn.

"I'll check it out," Lucky shouted. "Ned, Dusty, get on the hose. Spray the outside!"

Lucky peeled away toward the main house. Ned and Dusty pulled in the opposite direction, and Sarah and I skidded to a stop in front of Joe. My brother was bent over, coughing. He stood next to a pen with three frightened horses.

Joe pointed to the smoking barn. "There's one more in the back."

"That'll be Magic," said Sarah, jumping off of Hondo. She handed Hondo's reins to Joe and turned to me. "Let's go."

I jumped off of Harvey and handed his reins to Joe. "Keep breathing."

Joe held up a thumb and coughed again. I followed Sarah into the smoke-filled barn.

We crouched low as we walked inside. Rows of open stalls lined each side. Ahead of us, a column of bright-orange flames licked up the back left corner. The barn wasn't yet fully engulfed, but it wouldn't be long before the flames took over everything.

I could feel the heat as soon as we were inside. Panicked whinnies emanated from within the stall in the back right corner. Sarah stood long enough to snatch a rope from a hook on the wall. Then she dashed to the last stall on the right.

"Easy, girl." She unlatched the stall door and turned to me. "Take off your bandanna and cover her eyes."

I untied my bandanna and spread it open while Sarah reached in and attached the rope to Magic's halter. Wide-eyed, the horse jerked her head up in a panic.

"Whoa, girl. Easy, Magic," Sarah soothed her as she stroked the horse's head.

I coughed as I held my bandanna over the horse's eyes.

"Okay." Sarah backed up. "Here we go."

The three of us swiftly walked out of the smoke-filled barn. The horse still seemed frightened but not as panicked as before. I choked back a cough to keep the blindfold in place.

My throat was on fire as we finally reached the exit and emerged into the sweet, fresh air.

"I got her," Joe said as he ran up and took the lead from Sarah.

As the horse walked past, Sarah and I doubled over in coughing fits. A loud hiss erupted behind us. I turned and saw water sprinklers on the barn's rafters. They sprayed wide arcs of water, and the flames shrank back.

Lucky ran up to us. "Someone cut the power feed and the backup generator." He pointed to the back of the barn. "But that should kill the fire inside. I'll make sure Ned and Dusty have the outside covered."

Still coughing, Sarah just nodded.

As Lucky joined the others, Joe returned from the horse pen. "You two all right?"

Cough. "Just . . ." *Cough. Hack.* ". . . peachy," I replied.

Sarah coughed again and looked at Joe. "What happened?"

Joe told her about seeing the riders west of the ranch before he spotted smoke rising from the barn.

"I rang the bell because . . . isn't that what you do?" Joe shrugged. "And then I tried to get as many horses out as possible."

"Thank you," Sarah said, then turned back to the barn. Less smoke billowed out of the entrance, and the flames were completely gone.

Sarah shook her head. "I'm sick of this." She marched over to where Joe had tied their horses.

Joe and I exchanged glances.

Sarah untied Hondo, swung herself onto his back, and rode away at a gallop. At first she headed north, toward her father and the rest of the cattle drive. But then she swung west and kicked Hondo into a full run.

"Oh, boy," I said. She was after the culprits.

As one, Joe and I ran to our horses and climbed on. We urged them into a gallop, turning them westward. Not that she couldn't handle it, but we weren't about to let Sarah confront those guys alone.

BUSHWHACKED

16

JOE

FRANK AND I RODE AS FAST AS WE COULD but couldn't catch up to Sarah. Hondo was fast, and Sarah was more experienced. We kept her in sight as we trailed her westward.

"The motive was to slow us down," Frank announced.

I grinned. "Way ahead of you, bro. That's why I made it to the ranch so fast."

"So the bad guys just wanted to keep us away from the ranch so they could burn it down?" he asked.

"Sounds pretty stupid, if you ask me," I replied. "They could've beaten us here days ago. Why do all that other stuff?"

Up ahead, Sarah crested a rise and disappeared on the other side.

"Looks like Sarah's going to ask them personally," Frank said. "Alone."

"Yah!" I shouted, urging Norman faster.

As we topped the hill, we spotted Sarah in the distance. She slowed Hondo and walked him into a tree line before disappearing into the forest.

"We're losing her," Frank said.

We raced across the open field toward the place we'd last seen her. When we reached the trees, we slowed our horses and Frank took the lead. I followed him into the dense forest.

"Do you see her?" I asked.

"No," he replied.

I leaned out to look around him. "How about a trail?"

"Maybe." Frank nudged Harvey forward.

We snaked through the trees and dense undergrowth. We had to lean away and duck under low branches as we went. Our horses made one heck of a racket, snapping downed branches and crumpling dried leaves. It was a good thing we weren't trying to sneak up on her.

As we moved deeper into the woods, another sound rose to the surface—deep rumbling mixed with high-pitched whines. But I recognized the rhythmic beeps accompanying them—construction sounds. The beeps of heavy machinery in reverse.

The noises grew louder as we finally spotted Sarah. She stood on the ground beside Hondo, their backs to us. As we rode forward, she put up a hand.

"Careful," she warned. "We call this Widow Creek for a reason."

Frank and I climbed down from our horses and walked forward. There was a drop-off ahead—a big one. I leaned forward and noticed that we were standing atop a tall cliff. A tiny creek snaked along the ground at least one hundred feet below.

Beyond the creek was the source of the construction noises. Several large pieces of machinery were clearing the land, chopping trees. They worked together brutally but efficiently, slowly disassembling the forest below. The air was filled with the smell of diesel and freshly cut wood.

First, bulldozers would plow over small trees and underbrush, clearing wide paths to larger trees. Next, there were strange tractors with a horizontal set of pincers. The giant claw would clamp down on the lower part of the tree trunk and hold it in place. Then a huge chain-saw blade would emerge from the pincer and slice through the trunk. The tractor then lifted the severed tree and hauled it away.

"This was such a beautiful forest," Sarah said quietly. Her spirit seemed to have been sapped away by the desolate landscape below.

"What's going on?" I asked.

"Timber poachers," Sarah explained.

"I've heard of animal poachers but not timber poachers," Frank said.

Sarah nodded. "It's more common than you think. They

come onto people's property and cut as much timber as they can. It happens in state forests, national parks, and especially ranches that have tons of acres that they can't patrol all the time."

"Or on property where the owners will be gone for a while," Frank added.

I pointed to the equipment below. "There's the motive, right there. That's why someone wanted to slow us down."

"So let's stop them!" Frank cried.

Sarah sighed. "It's too late. They're almost done anyway. See?" She pointed to one of the tractors being loaded onto a long flatbed trailer.

"Well, we can at least report them," Frank suggested. "Maybe stop them from doing it to someone else."

I squinted at the trucks. "If I had binoculars, we could at least write down some plate numbers."

"Someone should have to pay," agreed Frank.

Sarah took a deep breath. "I know a way down there." She climbed onto her horse. "Let's go."

We followed Sarah as she rode along the cliff face. We wove through the woods, and soon the scene of the destruction was out of sight. Then Sarah turned back toward the cliff and disappeared from view. As Frank and I followed, we saw her riding down a thin, steep trail on the side of the cliff. Frank gave me a nervous glance as he urged his horse to follow. I steered Norman down last; all three of us leaned back in our saddles as we trotted over the steep grade.

Luckily, the horses were surefooted and we safely reached the creek below. Following Sarah's lead, we tied the horses to some smaller trees behind some scrub brush.

We crept through what was left of the forest, carefully making our way toward the unnatural clearing. We didn't have to worry about keeping quiet, since the loud noises masked our footsteps. We made our way to a massive tree on the edge of the clearing and huddled behind it. The thing had to be five feet wide—large enough to hide all three of us from view.

"This better?" Sarah whispered.

"Much." I reached into my pocket and pulled out my pen and notebook.

That's when a sharp *click* sounded behind us. I froze. It wasn't just any click. It was the kind I've heard in *all* my favorite westerns—the sound of the hammer being pulled back on a six-shooter. I hoped I was wrong as we slowly turned around.

But I wasn't.

Two masked cowboys stood three feet away, one aiming a large pistol at us.

17 SHOWDOWN

FRANK

I GLANCED AT MY BROTHER. "WHAT DO WE DO now, Cowboy Joe?"

Joe shrugged and slowly raised his hands. "Uh, reach for the sky?"

"That's right," said the man with the gun, who was wearing a black bandanna. "Nice and easy."

In our short, action-packed careers as detectives, Joe and I have faced this kind of scenario quite a few times. We never really get used to it, but the initial shock value had worn off.

"Mike? Tim?" asked Sarah. "Why are you doing this?"

The man wearing the red bandanna glanced nervously at his companion and then back at Sarah. "We don't know who you're talking about," he said nervously.

104

Sarah wasn't fazed. "Everyone knows you've been causing all this trouble. You're going to get caught eventually."

Black Bandanna pointed the barrel at Sarah. "First of all, no one's seen our faces. And second, if we *were* the two fellas you're talking about, I imagine that we'd have a nice alibi set up."

"A few cowhands on an out-of-state ranch who will swear we were with them the whole time," Red Bandanna added with a chuckle.

"Shut it!" Black Bandanna barked at him. He twirled the barrel of his pistol. "Turn around."

We did as we were told, and I found myself staring at thick tree bark.

"Uh, not very honorable to shoot someone in the back," Joe pointed out.

"We won't shoot you unless you try something," the man told us.

One of them grabbed my wrist and jerked it behind me. He pulled down my other arm, and I felt him tying my wrists together. Hard. "Hey!" I shouted.

"Quit your sniveling," he said.

After binding our wrists, they had us put our backs to the massive tree. Black Bandanna holstered his weapon, and they both wrapped a long rope around all three of us *and* the tree. After three tight loops, we were secured—Sarah in the middle with a Hardy on each side.

"Don't worry, someone will find you eventually," Black

Bandanna assured us. "We just have to cause a bit more mayhem on the other side of the ranch. Give our friends here plenty of time to clear out." He held up a finger. "Oh, and in case you do get free, we'll take your horses. It's a long walk back to the ranch. Everyone should be gone by then."

"How much are these poachers paying you?" asked Sarah.

Black Bandanna's eyes lightened. "A mighty nice finder's fee, thank you very much." He tipped his hat and they strode into the woods. They disappeared among the undergrowth.

Once they were out of sight, I struggled against my bonds. The ropes were tied so tightly that I could tell there was no way of wriggling out of them. My fingers already felt a bit numb.

I saw that Joe was busy doing the same. "Can you get loose?" I asked.

"Working on it," he replied. "But it doesn't look good."

"What do you mean?" I asked. "You always get loose first."

Joe grinned. "Not always. You get lucky sometimes."

Sarah's head spun to each of us, tracking the conversation. "Just how many times have you two been tied up?"

Joe rolled his eyes. "Let's see . . . too many to count, really."

"Yeah." I nodded. "It kind of comes with the territory."

Joe grinned. "We're actually in our element now."

Sarah was struggling between us but not as much. "How about you?" I asked. "Can you get free?"

"I'm not trying to get out of the ropes," she said. "I'm trying to reach my multi-tool."

Joe and I stopped moving.

"You have a multi-tool?" he asked. "The kind with pliers, a file . . ."

"And a knife?" I finished.

Sarah cringed as she twisted her body one last time. She relaxed and exhaled. "Yeah. But I can't reach it." She turned to me. "It's in a leather pouch on my belt, on my right side. Can you get to it?"

I turned away from her as far as the ropes across my stomach would allow. I reached my bound hands back and spread my fingers. They brushed against the small pouch. "I can feel it," I said.

I pushed closer and jabbed a finger under its flap. I felt it snap open. "Almost there." I stretched two fingers wide. "Got it."

"Hand it to me," Sarah instructed. "I know where the knife is."

"Okay." I stretched out my hands as Sarah's fingers reached for the tool. Now my fingers were already numb, and as I strained against the ropes, they got worse. So bad that I lost my grip on the tool. I felt it hit my ankle on the way down.

Sarah hadn't noticed. "Where is it?" Her fingers brushed against mine.

"Um . . . ," I started.

Joe sighed and hung his head. "You dropped it, didn't you?"

"Yeah, I kind of did," I replied.

"Aw, man," Joe said. "You always do that."

"I don't always do that," I replied. "The rope is too tight. My fingers are numb."

"Guys," Sarah said.

"Of course the rope is too tight," said Joe. "If it wasn't too tight, I'd be out by now."

"Guys, stop," Sarah ordered. But we didn't listen.

"You're the big Houdini fan," I said. "He would have escaped by now."

"Hey, don't bring the Big H into this," Joe sneered.

"Guys!" she yelled.

"What?!!" we shouted back.

She cocked her head. "Listen."

I had become used to the obnoxious construction noises behind us. But now, the rumbling and cracking grew louder. I leaned to the right and craned my neck to see. From my odd angle, I could barely get one eye to peek around the wide tree. I gasped when I spotted the bulldozer clearing a path toward us. Brush and dirt churned up in its path.

"It's a bulldozer," I reported. "And it's coming right for us."

"We're cool," said Joe. "A bulldozer can't knock down a tree this big."

My heart raced. "No, but the bulldozer just clears a path for that other thing, right? The thing with the claws and the built-in chain saw? You know, the one that cuts the tree at about"—I glanced back at the tree—"about where we are!"

Joe's eyes widened. "We're toast."

BUZZARD BAIT

18

JOE

I LEANED MY HEAD FORWARD AND SCANNED the ground. "Where's that multi-tool again?"

Frank and Sarah were already shuffling their feet, moving around dry leaves, trying to find the lost tool.

The rumbling behind us grew louder. Again, I turned, trying to glimpse the bulldozer behind us, but I couldn't see anything.

"I see it!" Frank shouted.

"Push it to my feet," Sarah told him. "I can pick it up."

I turned back to Sarah. "Really?"

"I think so," she told me. "I have an idea. Get your hands close to my side."

"Got it," I replied. I twisted to the left, jutting my bound hands as close to her as possible.

The stink of burning diesel thickened as the ground vibrated.

"Here it comes." Frank nudged the tool toward Sarah's feet.

She positioned the multi-tool between her boots and slowly lifted both feet off the ground, just as she had done during the rodeo. She grimaced as the ropes dug into her stomach. Once her feet were parallel to the ground, she kicked her legs up and released the tool. It arced up and landed on her shins.

"Way to go, gymnast trick rider," I shouted.

"Get ready," she croaked, her voice straining.

Sarah's body trembled as she raised her legs higher. The heavy tool began to slide along her jeans. It passed her knees and moved toward her thighs. Sarah grunted as she twisted her legs to the left and raised them even higher. Picking up speed, the tool slid across her left leg and into the air. I spread my fingers as wide as I could. . . .

"Got it!" I shouted.

Sarah's legs fell to the ground, and she gasped for air.

Suddenly the entire world seemed to shake as something slammed into the tree behind us. The tool nearly tumbled from my hands.

"What was that?" Sarah asked.

Frank leaned over. "The bulldozer. It hit the tree."

"Well, yell at the guy," I said. "Let him know we're here."

"Hey!" Frank yelled. "Help! We're trapped here! Hey!"

I ran my fingers over the tool. "Where's the knife on this thing?"

"It's on one of the sides," Sarah replied. "You don't have to open the pliers to get to it."

I closed my eyes and concentrated on finding the knife blade. Between the loud engines, the fuel smells, and the backup beeps, it was hard to focus.

"He's backing up," Frank reported. "He couldn't hear me. I think he's wearing ear protection."

I ran my fingers over the tool and pulled out one of its components. Sharp blade. Pointy tip. It was the knife. "I found it!"

"You better hurry," Frank warned. "Because I think the bulldozer's finished."

"No pressure," I said as I rotated the knife. The key was to cut the rope and not my skin. I'd done it before, just not with the looming threat of being sawed in half.

The trouble was I didn't just have to cut through the ropes holding my hands—I'd also have to cut through the thicker rope holding us to the tree.

"I think I see the big tractor coming," Frank reported.

"Help!" Sarah shouted. "Can anyone hear us?!!"

"Hey!" Frank joined her. "We're back here!"

I positioned the blade onto the rope and began to saw.

Here's a fact about cutting your way out of ropes. Depending on how you were tied up (what kind of knot, how many loops, etc.), you may have to cut through several strands, not just one. I couldn't really tell how the bandanna brothers had tied us. And even if I could, it would have been hard to remember between the vibrating ground, Frank and Sarah's yelling, and the threat of imminent death. I just hoped one strand would do the trick.

"How's it going, Joe?!!" Frank shouted. "It's almost here!"

"Just a second . . ." I sawed faster.

"I hope we have that long," Sarah said before going back to yelling at the driver.

I felt a release of pressure as I cut through the rope. Luckily, it only took one strand, and my hands were free. I arched my back and pulled my hands out from behind me. With the knife in my left hand, I went to work on the rope holding us to the tree.

"Joe?" Frank asked.

"Don't rush me!" I shouted as I sawed faster. The rope was thicker and hard to cut through.

The world shook again as something bigger hit the back of the tree. I was pushed forward against the ropes. The blade jostled away from the rope. I reached back to finish the cut.

Sarah screamed as the giant claws slammed onto either side of the tree. The knife trembled in my hand as I went back to work on the rope. A deafening whine filled the air as the chain saw powered up.

"Lean forward!" Frank ordered. I could barely make out what he said. "Push against the rope! Hard!"

The tip of the chain saw appeared on my side of the tree. I was barely halfway through the rope. I wasn't going to cut through in time. I closed my eyes and did as Frank instructed, lowering my head and pushing against the rope as hard as I could. Wood chips dusted my face as the chain saw began cutting the tree.

"Aaaaaah!" I screamed.

I had the sensation of falling just before something smacked me square in the face.

I opened my eyes to see that I was facedown on the forest floor. I scrambled onto my back and saw the strangest thing—the tree, standing straight up, floating away. It wasn't really floating; it just looked like it from my vantage point as the giant tractor backed away with its prize.

"Hey!" Frank shouted. "Is everyone okay?" His hands still tied behind his back, he struggled to roll off his face.

Sarah tried to sit up next to him. "What happened? How are we not cut in half?"

"When I saw where the thing clamped down on the tree, I knew that the built-in chain saw would cut the ropes as it sliced into the tree," Frank explained. "We would have had about half a second to get clear."

"That was too close," Sarah said.

"But close enough." I untied her hands. "I wasn't going to cut through in time." I gave her back the multi-tool.

Sarah closed the knife blade. "You should've used the blade with the serrated edge. Cuts through rope like butter."

"Now she tells me." I rolled my eyes. "I'll remember that the next time I'm in a similar situation."

She got to her feet. "If this happens to you as often as you say it does, you'd better remember."

I untied Frank and we followed Sarah back toward the creek. As promised, Norman, Harvey, and Hondo were missing. And I especially missed them as we waded through the cold creek and trudged up the steep cliff trail.

Once at the top, we turned to view the destruction once more. The last of the downed trees was being loaded, as well as the giant cutter, the one that almost sliced us in half. The poachers had finished stripping this part of the forest.

"By the time we make it back to the ranch, they'll be off the property," Sarah said. "They got away with it after all."

"Mike and Tim, too," I added. "Safe with their phony alibis."

Sarah turned and trudged through the woods toward the ranch. Frank and I followed in silence.

We stepped out of the tree line and were greeted by three men on horseback. We froze in our tracks. Mike and Tim scowled down at us, but that wasn't the surprising part. The rider in front wore a six-shooter and had an all-too-familiar face.

Sarah gasped. "Lucky?"

BRONC BUSTER

19

FRANK

AT FIRST I WASN'T SURPRISED TO
see Lucky with the two masked bandits.
After all, we'd suspected him of being
involved with them somehow. But as I
quickly took in the scene, some things
didn't quite fit. The bandanna brothers no longer hid their
faces. Neither one of them wore a gun belt. Lucky was the
only one with a six-shooter. And both Mike and Tim had
their hands tied in front of them.

"Heard you ran into a little trouble," Lucky said with a
grin.

"Hey!" Joe said. "You caught the bad guys!"

Lucky nodded. "That I did."

"How?" I asked.

"After the fire was out, I tracked you to Widow Creek." He jutted a thumb over his shoulder. "I caught these two heading out with your horses."

"But they were armed," Sarah said.

"Oh, it took a little persuading." Lucky smiled. "But I got them to give themselves up and tell me about their side job for some poachers."

I noticed that one of them had the beginnings of a black eye. The other had a split lip and a swollen nose. Joe must've seen the same thing.

"That's what I'm talking about," he said. "Real cowboy stuff right there! Tracking . . . fisticuffs . . ." He held up both fists.

"Fisticuffs?" I raised an eyebrow at my brother. "Really?"

Joe grinned and nodded. "Oh, yeah."

"Got your horses over there." Lucky pointed farther down the tree line, where Harvey, Norman, and Hondo were tied to a tree.

I felt a twang of guilt for suspecting Lucky. Lucky was one of the good guys.

"I wish we could've caught the poachers, too," Sarah said.

"I wouldn't worry about them," Lucky reassured us. "I just got off the phone with the sheriff's department. By the time those trucks hit the west gate, there'll be a couple of deputies waiting for them."

"Wait. What happened to no cell phones on the trail?" Joe asked.

"That's just for the tourists." Lucky reached into his shirt pocket and pulled out a smartphone. "Besides, you know how many good cowboy apps I have? Campfire recipes, a compass, knot tutorials, stargazing . . . I love memorizing constellations."

I grinned at Joe. "Real cowboy stuff."

Lucky laughed. "*Modern* cowboy stuff."

The three of us mounted up and rode back to the ranch. Once there, Lucky turned Mike and Tim over to a sheriff's deputy. Sarah, Joe, and I gave statements that added a bunch of charges that went way beyond mere timber poaching and sabotage. After all that ugly business was taken care of, Wally came through with his promise of cowboy barbecue.

Like the previous meals, everyone gathered to eat and share stories about the day's adventures. Except this time, there was the entire cattle drive to discuss, not to mention our adventure at Widow Creek.

Wally's cooking was excellent as usual; there was barbecued brisket, chicken, pork ribs, corn on the cob, and beans.

After the meal, Wally put his arms around our shoulders. "Boys, I want to thank you for your hard work," he said. "Cowhand-wise *and* detective-wise. If you ever want to hit the trail with us again, you just say the word."

"Way cool!" Joe said. It was clear he would do it all again in a heartbeat.

"Thanks," I said. I had to admit that I'd had a better time

than I thought I would. Who knows, maybe after some time passed—and after it no longer hurt to sit down—I might consider doing something like this again.

"I'm just sorry we couldn't stop them from clearing your forest," I told him.

Wally nodded. "Yeah, me too. But the responsible parties will pay, the land will eventually recover, and who knows, maybe we stopped them from doing it to the next rancher down the line."

"I hope so," I agreed.

Wally looked at his watch. "We'll be shuttling everyone back to Bayport in about an hour. Don't forget your gear in the chuck wagon." He winked. "You might get to use those sleeping bags someday."

Wally moved to the other guests as Joe and I made our way toward the chuck wagon.

"I can't wait to sleep in my own bed," I said. "Under a roof, with electricity . . ."

"And the Internet," Joe added.

"Oh, yeah," I agreed.

Sarah intercepted us. "I know my dad already thanked you, but I want to thank you too."

Joe tipped his hat. "Shucks, ma'am. 'Tweren't nothin'."

I winced. "Did you just say *'tweren't*?"

Sarah laughed. "We've had many . . . *different* guests over the years. But you made this cattle drive quite memorable." She locked eyes with me.

Okay, this was the part where Joe was supposed to get the hint and walk away. But did he? No.

Joe laughed and crossed his arms. "Yeah, how many dirt bike cattle rustlers do you get on these things?"

Luckily, Dusty and Ned strolled up to Joe and took care of my problem.

"There he is," Ned told him.

Dusty twirled his toothpick as he clapped a hand onto Joe's shoulder. "Just the man we want to see."

Ned nodded. "That's right. Before you go, how would you like to try your hand at bronc busting?"

"Like in the rodeo?" Joe asked. "For real?"

"Yep," said Dusty. "And we happen to have just the meanest, most ornery beast you've ever seen."

Joe rolled his eyes. "What's his name? Wendell? Oliver? Fred?"

Ned shook his head. "Uh-uh." A grin spread across his face. "Diablo."

Joe clapped his hands together and grinned at me. "See? That's what I'm talking about!"

After Joe left with the two ranch hands, I smiled at Sarah. "So, uh . . . good luck at college. I'm glad I got to hang out with you before you left."

Sarah glanced down and smiled. "Text me sometime," she said. "I'll be back for holidays and spring break. Maybe you can come visit the ranch again. Ride another cattle drive."

I nodded. "Yeah, sure. Or . . ." I shrugged. "You know

Bayport is lovely around the holidays. If you ever want to have a non-horseback, non-camping adventure in the city . . ."

Sarah laughed. "I get it. That sounds fun too." She leaned in and kissed me on the cheek. "Now, come on." She took my hand and led me toward the main corral. "You don't want to miss this."

Everyone was gathered around the large circular stockade. Some sat atop the wooden fence, while others peered through the slats. Across from us, I saw Ned and Dusty working in an adjoining stall. They helped my brother climb onto a large black horse.

"Just how dangerous is this?" I asked Sarah. "My mom would kill me if I returned my brother with any broken limbs."

She pointed to the center of the enclosure. "The whole pen is filled with a thick layer of fluffy soil. It's very soft, actually."

I swallowed hard as Ned hopped over the fence and reached for the gate. He swung it open and the black horse jumped out. Everyone cheered as Joe hung on for dear life. He held one arm out as he rode the bucking bronco. I was surprised at how well my brother was doing.

"Is Diablo holding back or something?" I asked. The horse was definitely trying to throw Joe, but the animal didn't seem to leap as high or buck as violently as some of the horses we'd seen in the rodeo.

"It won't feel like that to Joe," she replied. "Or look that way in the pictures." She nodded up to Lucky. The cow-hand had his smartphone out and was busy photographing the event.

Sarah grinned. "Ned and Dusty always find someone to ride . . . Diablo at the end of each cattle drive. He's very safe."

I caught her pause before she mentioned the horse's name. "Wait a minute. His name isn't really Diablo, is it?"

Sarah grinned. "No. It's Cupcake."

I laughed. "Please don't tell Joe. It'll break his heart."

We cheered with the others as my brother rode on.